# VENUS
## AND
# MARS

# PATRICK J. JONES

# VENUS
## AND
# MARS

Published by Patrick J. Jones
Red Hook, N.Y. 12571
Phone : 617-785-8559
annandale17 @ aol.com

VENUS AND MARS

Printed In The United States of America
Charleston SC


ISBN: 9781452801070


Cover photography – Patrick J. Jones

# Forward and Dedication

The idea for this book came to me in 2005 while living in Boston. Over the period of about a week, I experienced a series of recurring dreams that have haunted me ever since. Every time I would wake from my sleep, I remembered vivid details of the images that ran through my head while I slept. I have not experienced any part of the dreams again since then. I wrote down pages of notes here and there about what happened and in 2007 started to construct them and the memories into this story.

The beginning of the book is a factual account of my life up until the point when the dream started. I have included this information to provide the reader with an accurate timeline of how things really were in my life before the summer of 1981.

I developed a unique style of writing in order to tell this story. I felt it should be very informal. There are no page numbers or chapter breaks. The dialog is full of contractions, fragments, and passive voice. The main characters even lack description. After all, we are talking about a series of dreams that developed into a story. I think it works quite well. Having said that, I still feel that you will be moved by the story, even though I have broken every literary rule on the way to get you there.

My actual life could not have ended up more different from the story in this book. The series of dreams that I had, created by my subconscious mind, have many personal messages for me. I dedicate this story to all those who suffered directly and indirectly from my addiction…family, relationships, friends, employers, and victims.

I would like to thank Mark Reichelt and his wife Evie, for giving me their help in the final days of putting this book together. A extra special thanks to Lana and her entire family in Boston, without their love and support at such a trying time in my life, I would not be here to tell this story. Oh, and Lana, thanks for letting me borrow your first name for the main character in the story.

By the time I turned seventeen, I had committed enough crime to warrant a life sentence in prison. If you asked me, I was on my way to the big time. If you asked my parents, I was on my way to the big house. I was the neighborhood thief, drug addict, vandal, and well rounded juvenile delinquent. I wasn't raised to be like this. My parents, as well as local law enforcement, were going crazy trying to figure out what to do with me.

The way I saw it, everyone was making a big fuss over nothing. In retrospect, I had arrived at the point where I could no longer tell the difference between right and wrong. If everyone would just leave me alone everything would be fine. It was obvious to everyone except me that I was out of control, spinning further into a life of drug addiction and lost chances.

I would have died before I ever admitted there was a problem. I had an answer for everything. I was never wrong. I had no intentions of changing one single bit. For all I cared they could lock me up and throw away the key. Then I met her. Her name was Lana Myers. That was the exact moment the metamorphosis started. We went to the same high school and that seemed like the only thing we had in common. We were on opposite ends of the spectrum.

Lana was involved in music, sports, after school activities, and was one of the brightest in our class. Added to that, she was also one of the yearbook photographers. I would have to say that she was well liked by everyone. She lacked the air of conceit, like some girls of her caliber. In my eyes, she was perfect. In the small gang of hoodlums that I ran with, I had nicknamed her Venus even though I had never so much as spoken a word to her.

Me on the other hand, spent most of the days at school cutting classes, getting high, gambling, or dealing drugs. My character was not lacking, but my actions kept most people at a distance. It was common knowledge that I was a frequent visitor to the principal's office as well as the local police station. When we met and started talking at the local hospital, surely I was dreaming…

# Part One
# Fact
# Real Life

I was born just outside the Akwesasne reservation in the small town of Ogdensburg, New York. My mother put me up for adoption at the age of six months. From what my adopted parents have told me, my mother was full-blooded Native American from the Mohawk tribe. No information was ever given to me about my father. At the time of my birth, my mother was already raising four children. She was not married and could not handle another infant. St. Lawrence County Department of Social Services handled the adoption. My mother, who was living on the reservation in 1964, felt that adoption was the best choice to ensure that I had a life full with opportunity. The reservation had a very high rate of alcoholism and drug addiction. According to my parents, my birth mother may have been one of the many afflicted with the disease.

My adopted parents had tried several times to have children after their marriage in 1955. After several painful miscarriages, they decided to adopt children. By the time the sixties rolled around, my father had established himself in a military career. My mother had completed her nurses training and now was a registered nurse. When all was said and done, they would adopt three children. I would have an older brother and a younger sister. With my father's career, we would end up traveling across the United States as well as overseas.

My earliest memories are of living in New Mexico. We were stationed at Clovis Air Force base. My parents were raising us catholic, so my first school was Sacred Heart. I was very bright if the subject interested me, but more often than not, I was disruptive in class.

The nuns had their hands full with me pulling the girls pigtails, making noise, or picking my nose and finding creative places to wipe it. Needless to say, I sat in the corner a lot with my hands folded. I had my hands slapped with a ruler. My mouth was closed with a piece of tape. Nobody was going to stop me from picking my nose though. It was a typical catholic upbringing in the late sixties. No harm done.

For my next few years of school, my father was transferred to Addis Ababa, the capitol of Ethiopia in Africa. Now this was really something. We lived in a very modern compound of houses with other families who were recently stationed over there due to Nixon's foreign policy. I remember everything about growing up in Africa. We lived in a nice house with a high wall that surrounded the property. There was a large iron gate in the front. We had several animals as pets. Our two guard dogs protected us by roaming around the property or keeping watch from the gatehouse. Their hind legs were much shorter than their front ones and my father told us they were part hyena. We also had a horse, birds, cats, turtles, and rabbits.

We also owned two monkeys. One was a green monkey and the other was a fun loving chimpanzee. His name was Cheetah. He was almost never on his chain. He walked around the property like one of us. He liked to walk holding hands or he rode on our shoulders. I will never forget the time the compound was raided by red army ants. A sea of them marched across the front yard toward the house. My brother and me were outside. The ants got into our hair and clothes.

We ran into the house dancing in pain. We looked like we were stepping on hot coals. Cheetah was also let inside because it was too late to put him in his cage. He took turns sitting on our shoulders and began grooming us for ants, eating them as he went along. We were crying from the ant bites and laughing at the same time because of the antics of our monkey. Priceless.

Our House was always full of maids and servants. These people were the locals who earned their living taking care of our home and the animals. They lived in mud huts with thatched roofs. These simple homes dotted the landscape around the military compound. It was clear that poverty was just outside our wall. This was the Ethiopia that the world envisioned. I was too young to really understand it. In the heart of the capitol city, there were high-rise buildings of modern day companies and the hustle and bustle of any large city in the world. Ethiopia was far from poor. There was also the palace of Ethiopia's great emperor Haile Selassie. I remember many visits to this great edifice. On one visit, where he was honoring the U.S. troops, the great man shook all of our hands. I did not know who he was then, but as we grew up my mother often talked of this notable event.

I was filled with so many unique experiences growing up in Africa. One thing in particular that stuck in my mind was how large the full moons were. Living on the equator, you could see the surface craters in detail with your naked eye. It was as if you could reach out and touch it. The other thing that was memorable as a child was all of the animals that were native to the area. I saw alligators, giant snakes,

Nile perch, anteaters, zebras, hippos, lions, and a host of other animals long before I ever stepped foot in a zoo.

When there was a lack of interesting things to see and do, I created my own. School was one of those places. I was hell on wheels without the nuns to watch me. The doctors in Africa diagnosed me with hyperactivity and I was placed on Ritalin to calm me down. After a little over a year, my mother made the decision to take me off it. She was hearing about the side effects of this widely used drug and decided it was too dangerous for me. Once again, I became easily bored at school, which usually led to me being disruptive.

My father's time in Ethiopia ended after a few years and we were transferred back stateside to Rome, New York. After a short time in Rome, my father retired and we settled in Rhinebeck. I would spend grades four through seven there and form some of my closest bonds with a small group of friends. Making friends when you were young was easy enough; you just walked up to anyone and started playing. Friends were a dime a dozen. At this point in my life, I noticed a little pressure and fear about whether or not I would fit in with my peers. Later down the road, it would be these feelings that would end up being the straw that broke the camels back.

My lighthearted disposition and mischievousness landed me four of the closest friends I have ever had. I grew more into the class clown than the unruly student during these preteen years. My main interests were sports and my friends. My parents were more than happy to see an outlet for my energy and were content with driving me back and forth. My father and I became very close during Little

League. He never missed a game. I really think he enjoyed it more than I did. I settled into this comfort zone of baseball, swim meets, television, slumber parties, and recess periods.

All of this would come to an abrupt end when my father accepted a manager's position with the propane company he worked for. We would be moving to Londonderry, New Hampshire and my life was over. I would be starting high school over in a strange new place. I would have to make a whole new set of friends. At twelve years old, I was scared to death. Puberty, fear, and worry would wreck havoc on my nerves before we even left New York. Moving to a new location took on a very sinister face this time. I protested, screamed and threw myself on the floor to no avail. No such luck. We would be moving and I was counting the days to my demise.

I was filled with so much anxiety that something inside me snapped. Dr. Jekell was about to turn into Mr. Hyde. I said goodbye to my friends and off we went. It was summer. We found a house and settled in. I would not come out of my room. My mother insisted that I get out and make some new friends. "There were boys my age all over the neighborhood," she kept repeating. After almost a full month of summer wasted indoors, I finally ventured out into the light.

Many of the kids that I met in the area were experimenting with alcohol and drugs. I eventually had my very first drink and found my calling. I felt as if I fit right in, all of my worries vanished with a few swallows out of a bottle. I drank so much that I was sick for hours. I was heaving up my insides all over the woods on a hot summer day. A normal person would have had enough. I could not wait to do it again. When school started, I had no fears or worries. I was gulping down my parents booze at six in the morning before the first day of school.

By the time my freshman year rolled around, I was reckless, experimenting with every drug except heroin. People that used heroin were junkies and had all kinds of problems. I did not have a problem. During my freshman year, I started breaking into houses to support my drug addiction. I started buying LSD and horse tranquilizers 100 doses at a time. If there were any other types of pills for sale at school, I would buy a small supply for my own use. I was smoking a half-ounce of pot a week as well. I was a mess in everyone's eyes, but my own.

I found a friend, Chris DeMenna, who would sometimes rob houses with me. He was a few years older than me and had his license. He was my fence. He would drive me into the city and pawn our gold, silver and jewels. You could drop Chris off in the Amazon jungle with a bag of stolen loot and he would show up at your house the next day with a million dollar smile and a pocket full of cash. I had money to burn on whatever I wanted. I was living the high life. The first time my parents suspected anything was when my mother found some marijuana in my dresser drawer. Things went quickly down hill from there.

She was looking for a watch battery for my father's watch that had stopped running. I kept my pot in a plastic Timex watchcase that I stored in my top dresser drawer. My mother must have seen this case a thousand times because my socks and underwear were also in there and she washed, folded, and put away the family laundry. She opened the watch box expecting to find a battery and came across my stash.

I remember her yelling for me up and down the neighborhood like a wild woman. My friends and I had never seen anything like it. The fact that we were stoned silly when she pulled up in the family car screaming her lungs out did not help much. I followed her home on my bike after my friends all did their imitations of her as soon as she drove out of earshot. When I walked through the living room door, my father was propped up in a chair at the dining room table. My mother was seated across from my dad furiously unrolling several joints in a large glass ashtray. I can remember they were rolled in strawberry rolling papers, so they were pink. The look on my face as I approached the kitchen table must have been priceless.

"What in the hell is this?" My mother said, as I approached the table.

"I don't know," I managed.

"Well if you don't know, just who in Gods green earth does?" My father snorted.

"Why are your eyes so bloodshot?" My mom asked next.

I could feel the Visine bottle resting in my pocket, along with the pipe that I used when I wasn't smoking joints. I couldn't think of a single thing to say, so I just stared at my sneakers and prayed that one of them wasn't going to ask me to empty my pockets.

"Where did you get it?" My mother screamed.

"I'm holding it for a friend," I offered.

As I glanced up, I could see that she was finished tearing up the items in question and her fingertips were a dull rose color from the papers. She brought the ashtray to her nose and took a sniff, looked at my father, and then took another good sniff.

"I think that's marijuana!" My mother shouted.

"Jesus H. Christ," he replied to her diagnosis. "Son, now just what in the hell have you got yourself mixed up in?"

I could not utter a single word in reply, so I went back to my sneakers and slowly put my hands in my pockets to try to hide the bulges of paraphernalia. The silence seemed to last for an eternity while my mother continued to smell the pile of green powder in the ashtray. Out of the corner of my eye, I could see her raise the tray to her nose and then shake her head in disbelief. She repeated this action several times, as a wine connoisseur would breathe in the bouquet of a vintage glass of Chablis. After each shake of her head, she would glance at my father, and then turn her eyes on me. I must have been white as a ghost standing there waiting for my parents to finish holding court at the kitchen table.

"Young man, you go to your room until we figure out what to do about this," my father said.

"Am I grounded?" I squeaked out, as I hurried past them toward my room.

I had to move quick when my father sent me to my room because more often than not, he was an obstacle in the way and you were sure to get a slap to the back of the head or a good foot to the ass as you went by him.

Inside my room, I breathed a sigh of relief and made a quick inventory of all my other drugs, even though I knew if any of them had been found, things would have turned out much worse. I sat on the edge of my bed and looked around. Being sent to my room was not so bad after all because even though my mother cried poverty all of the time, I had everything I ever wanted or needed including television, stereo, and video games. My parents did an excellent job of providing for my brother, sister, and me on a limited budget.

I ended up being grounded for a month, but it made no difference because I would climb out my window at night as soon as my mother went to work at the hospital. She worked an 11 to 7 shift some nights at the hospital. By the time she went to work on those nights, my father would be fast asleep. I would climb out my window, ride off on my bicycle, and look for houses to rob or meet up with friends. On the weekend, we would pass the early morning hours getting stoned and robbing houses, cars, or construction sites.

Before I knew it, I was in trouble with school, the police, and the local courts. My parents were pulling their hair out wondering what had happened to their sweet little boy. I was up to my eyeballs in quicksand. I was banned from ever playing sports for my school. I was kicked off the baseball team before the first game ever started. I didn't take all of this very well and spun out of control. I was convicted of several felony charges of Breaking and Entry. I was thrown in the Youth Development Center. I was also put on probation, as it was my first time before the local court system. It did not slow me down at all.

I started selling LSD and tranquilizers and made my money that way. Over the next year or so, there was a steady increase in my drug use. It got to the point where I was in so much trouble at school that I was going to be expelled if they ever caught me with drugs again. I wiggled my way around probation by tampering with my urine tests. My parents found another house in town and we moved. The first sign of trouble was when my mother found a mop bucket full of gold and silver under the addition to our house. She tossed all of it into the brook that ran behind our house. At least the fish would be eating well. From that point on she would tear up my room looking for drugs on a regular basis.

When my mother did find drugs, she would call the local police on me. Sometimes, I was guilty by suspicion, which also resulted in a phone call to the authorities. The detectives and my parents were on a first name basis. My fingerprints were being checked against all of the burglaries in town. It was only a matter of time until I was arrested again. I had left fingerprints all over a house I robbed and the police picked me up quickly afterward. I ended up face to face with the same judge who had previously warned me about re-appearing in front of him again for this type of tomfoolery. Yes, he actually used that word.

I could not be tried as an adult, so I don't think it fazed me one bit. As long as I was stoned or high, nothing really bothered me. It was like water off a ducks back. My parents were instructed not to let me go anywhere after school or weekends. I was on house arrest. I had a major stash of booze, pills, and drugs, so what did I care? I also had a flawless hiding spot from my mother…the fish tank. I didn't really have a clue how much I was hurting those who loved me. When guilt reared its ugly head, I just used more drugs to make it all go away. At some point, I began to use drugs to feel comfortable in my own skin. I really couldn't stand myself. If someone else were treating my family the way I was, I would have shot them with one of my friends guns. No questions asked, right between the eyes.

The day of sentencing came along with the close of my junior year. It was June and it was hot. Everyone dressed up in his or her best clothes and off we went to the courthouse. I was stoned and a little too smug for my mothers liking. What was the worst they could do to me? Slap me on the hands again? Ouch. No sir, I promise I will not do that again…as if that was going to do anything.

In my defense, my mother pleaded her case of "How could this have happened?" to the judge. The local police verified that I was from a good family. They mentioned how bright I was when I applied myself at school. I was the product of drug addiction. The judge stared at me from over his glasses and wagged his crooked finger at me. He gave me a second break and sentenced me to probation until my eighteenth birthday, restitution, and community service. As an added bonus, I was to attend the Scared Straight Program tour of the State Prison facility in Concord, New Hampshire. Boo hoo. Big deal. Can we all go home now, so I can get stoned? You're all stupid little fools. If you only knew.

# Part Two
# Fiction
# The Dreams


Probation was changed to every other week instead of once a month. My new probation officer would also be randomly drug testing me. Restitution was several thousand dollars and I would have to find a job after school. My community service was to be served at a nearby hospital. I would volunteer my services both Saturday and Sunday. I was to report for a full week of training at the hospital kitchen on the first Monday after school ended. I would be helping the dietary aides by picking up the meal trays in the various patient rooms throughout the hospital. So what…at least it would get me out of the house.

If I could pull the wool over my parents eyes for a little while perhaps everything would be forgotten. My brother had enlisted in the Air Force and left his car behind for me to use provided I remained on the straight and narrow. I managed to find a job at a local restaurant a few nights a week washing dishes. School ended and summer vacation started. I had almost a thousand dollars hidden from the robberies. I had no intentions of really changing, but I would have to put on one hell of a show to get everyone off my back. Little did I know that on the first day of training at the hospital every plan I had in my head would be turned upside down.

It was a sweltering day in mid June. My parents had decided on not letting me use my brother's car. They wanted to see results first. My mother dropped me off in front of the hospital. I was to report to the kitchen supervisor at four forty-five on the dot. It was four thirty. I waved goodbye and walked in and right back out the front door. I went to the far end of the parking lot and lit up a joint. After getting high, I popped some gum into my mouth and gave my eyes the Visine douche. Ready to rumble. I went inside, found my way to the cafeteria, and asked for Mr. Schwab, he was in charge of the kitchen.

I was directed to his office. He informed me that I would be training for the first week. I was going to be following one of the workers around and picking up dinner trays and then loading them on the carts. The carts would be brought down to the kitchen, so the trays could be washed and stacked for the next meal. Easy enough. He gave me a brief tour of the kitchen and cafeteria and introduced me to the people I would be working with. I was assigned a locker and was handed an apron. We would be picking up trays from the first location in five minutes.

The Intensive Care Unit was the first stop on our rounds and that is where we first met. I was wearing blue jeans and a black concert tee shirt, so except for the linen apron that I was told to put on, I thought I looked good. I had no idea what was waiting for me just down the hall. John, my trainer, was meticulous in his instructions.

"Do not bother the patients. Respect their privacy. Don't touch anything except the tray. Speak only when spoken to. Put the lids on in the right direction."

Blah. Blah. Blah. Blah.

"The I.C.U. has fifteen private rooms," John started again. "These patients could be very sick, so do not disturb them."

"Okay," I said, looking around.

"I will start here. You can go all the way down to the far end. The last room is on the left."

"Gotcha," and off I went.

I could see several patients hooked up to machines. Instruments were buzzing and whirling. Bad art was mixed with shiny floors. I could smell cleaning fluids. I walked past the nurses station to the last room on the left. I entered the room and glanced up and there she was. Venus. She was sitting on top of the bed reading a book. She looked up at me and put the book down.

"What are *you* doing here?"

She caught me off guard…I stammered for something to say.

"I'm um"…I froze.

"You're um what? C'mon whole words now…you can do it."

"I'm here to pick up the tray."

"Do you work here?"

"Not exactly."

"Not exactly what? Can I get one straight answer out of you?"

She almost smiled. I could tell she was pulling my leg.

"I'm kind of like a volunteer here."

"You a volunteer. Now that's funny. Have you been smoking that stuff you sell all day long in school?"

She was really letting me have it.

"Excuse me. Did I say that out loud? I'm so sorry."

She let out a little giggle and looked right at me. I couldn't think of anything witty to say back to her, so I reached for the tray on the bedside table.

"I haven't even eaten yet, and you want to whisk my tray away?"

I pulled my hands back and looked at her. She was the prettiest thing I had ever seen.

"Fine. I will leave it then," I said, looking at her.

"The food is terrible here…it's all yours."

She picked up the apple off the tray and bit into it. I couldn't help myself; I just stood there and stared at her.

"I've seen you around in school," she said. "We are both in the same class. Patrick Fisher isn't it?"

Before I could answer, she continued.

"You hang with all of the burnouts. What are you…the leader of the pack?"

I could see she was enjoying this, so I figured I would give it right back to her.

"Do you have a personal problem with me or just the food? There is a complaint department downstairs lady."

I gave her a sly smile and lifted the tray off the table. She took another bite of her apple and studied me in between chews.

"Don't you recognize me from school?" She said in a friendlier tone.

I answered a little too quickly and Freud got the best of me.

"Sure you're Venus…I mean Lana Meyers."

Oh crap, I was in trouble. I must have looked like a Bob's Big Boy statue standing there holding the tray.

"Venus? Who in the heck is Venus?"

I just stood there looking at her, faithfully holding the tray.

"You must really be out in the stratosphere tonight. Earth to Patrick? Hello? Is there anybody home?"

She snapped her fingers a couple of times.

"Can you cool it with the drug jokes?" I asked in my defense.

She did her best impression of someone smoking a joint. She took a big drag with her face all scrunched up, faked a snort and a cough, and pretended to pass me the imaginary joint.

"Here dude," she said, holding in her breath.

She burst out laughing. It was so funny I had all I could do to compose myself. I just shook my head and smiled right back at her.

"Patrick is there a problem?" John said from the doorway. "I have collected every tray on the unit."

He looked at Lana.

"I'm sorry Miss," John said in an apologetic tone.

She saw the opportunity to finish me off.

"You should keep your dog on a shorter leash Mister."

She looked at me and made a slight face.

"Do you two know each other?" John said.

"We are in the same class at school," I said.

"Yeah, when he shows up," she added.

"Cool it Venus."

I did it again.

"Lana," she raised her voice. "The name is Lana Meyers."

"Whatever," I shot back at her.

I spun around with the tray and headed for the door. John left the room ahead of me. I turned back toward her before I started down the hall. John was watching my every move. She was standing by the bed now with a camera in her hand. She took my picture.

"Yes Mars?" She grinned. "If I'm Venus then you're Mars," she said.

I took the bait.

"Why Mars?" I asked.

"Because, you're a real space cadet!"

She laughed and took another picture. She was wearing sweat pants and a pink polo shirt. She started to twirl her hair with her finger, camera hanging around her neck. She seemed to have a glow all around her. She was gorgeous.

"I have to go," I said.

"Oh Mars, will you please stop by later? It was so much fun meeting you...really," she said in her best southern belle voice.

"Sure," I said, as John cleared his throat.

During John's second lecture on patient etiquette, I was thinking about Lana being a patient in the Intensive Care Unit. She seemed fine. What could possibly be wrong with her? I was going to ask John and thought better of it. I managed to get through the rest of the rooms without incident. I could not get my mind off Lana. I kicked things around in my head the entire time John showed me how to run the dishwasher. After an hour, I started to feel nervous about the whole situation. She was making fun of me. She must really be laughing it up right about now. All of the trays were washed and stacked for the morning; my last duty was to take the trash out.

I finished with a half hour left before my father would arrive to pick me up. I went back out to the parking lot again. I smoked a quick joint and got high. Suddenly I had the courage to check up on Lana. I needed to find out if everything was all right with her. I made my way back to her room and poked my head in her doorway. She was in a chair reading a book. I glanced around at all of the equipment around the room. She didn't appear to be monitored by any of it.

"Hello," I finally said.

"Oh hi Mars, come on in," she said, putting the book down.

Her tone was very neutral. I took a couple of steps into the room.

"I stopped back up here to make sure you're doing well. What brings you to the hospital?"

"My doctor wants me to spend a few days here, so they can run some tests on me. I have been getting these awful headaches on and off for the last year or so. He has not been able to figure out what's causing them."

"Why the I.C.U. unit?"

"Tonight I have to sleep with this monitor attached to my head."

She pointed to a machine near the bed.

"Looks like an awful lot of equipment for a few headaches," I said, glancing around the room.

"Well, my parents and doctor want to check everything. You know how that goes."

"Yeah, I guess."

"When are you working, or should I say, volunteering again?"

"Tomorrow, five to nine."

"Stop in and see me?"

"Sure."

"Good," she smiled. "Then you can explain who Venus is. You can also tell me about the volunteer work that you're doing here at the hospital. It's so not you."

"I will."

"Come by after you're finished, visiting will be over by then and my parents will be gone. Now I have to get ready for bed and call the nurse to come attach all of this equipment on me."

"Okay, I'll see you then. My father will be out front in a few minutes."

She stood up and went over to the table by the bed. She picked up her camera.

"One more picture before you leave?"

"Oh no you don't."

"I'll show all of your buddies at school the pictures I took earlier. I'm sure they don't know that you're moonlighting as a volunteer here at the hospital."

"Alright, one picture."

She took two and put the camera back on the table.

"You know I was just kidding earlier. I hope I didn't get you into any trouble."

"You gave it to me pretty good."

"You deserve it. You're such a little troublemaker in school."

"Who me?" I said, and gestured to myself.

We both laughed. I looked right into her eyes and she started to twirl her hair.

"Do you need anything before I leave?"

"No, I think I'm all set. Would you let them know at the desk that I'm ready for them now?"

"Sure, then I guess I will see you tomorrow?"

"That would be great. Goodnight Mars," she said, sitting down on the edge of the bed.

"Goodnight Venus," I said, and turned to walk out of the room.

"You are really something else," she said.

"You ain't seen nothing yet," I replied, and walked out the door.

I walked to the nurses desk and let them know she was ready to be hooked up to the monitors. I took the elevator downstairs and went out the front door where my father was waiting for me in the car. I don't even remember the ride home with my father. Every thought in my head was about Lana. Never did I think the day would come when we would say two words to each other. In school if I saw her coming down the hallway toward me, I would get so nervous about saying hello to her. I would end up looking at my feet as we passed each other. I had no confidence in myself. Now I felt embarrassed that she knew about the drugs. I wished for the first time in my life that things were different.

On the ride home, I concluded that she was just being nice to me. We were in the same class in school, that's all it was. She was friendly with everyone. Somewhere in my heart, I longed for something different with her. There was this exhilarating feeling running through my veins. It felt better than any high drugs ever gave me. I couldn't put my finger on it. Oh, whom was I kidding? I was like a lovesick puppy dog. I was crazy about her. I knew it the moment I first saw her taking pictures for the yearbook. Now that the ice was broken, I wanted to be around her more than anything in the world. I couldn't wait to see her again.

When we arrived home, I went down to my room and had a few gulps of whisky. I needed to calm down and think. As soon as the booze hit me, I regretted it almost immediately. No wonder I had yet to experience my first romantic encounter. I was so afraid of being turned down and rejected that I couldn't even talk to girls. Around my friends I felt safe, but I was so lonely. I took another sip out of the bottle. The more I drank, the worse I felt. For the first time in my life, I wasn't able to run away from my feelings with booze or drugs.

What chance did someone like me have with a girl like Lana anyway? I was fooling myself if I thought our relationship would go anywhere. She would be the laughing stock of the entire school if she were seen with me. I had nobody to blame except myself. Where did all of this get me anyway? I was going to be a senior next year and I was still a virgin. I put the bottle away and went to bed.

When I woke in the morning, I could hear my father getting ready for work upstairs. I opened the back door. I listened to the brook flowing behind our house. It was bright outside, the start of a perfect summer day. I couldn't wait for my mother to get home from work to drive me to the hospital. I was in for a long day. My mother would be calling several times during the day to make sure I didn't leave to go anywhere. I couldn't really blame her. I spent the day watching television and getting high. Finally, my mother came home and drove me to the hospital after she got dinner started.

I arrived at the hospital with forty-five minutes to spare. It was the new routine again, go in and right back out the front door, get stoned, and go back inside. I went straight to Lana's room and a new patient was in there. My heart dropped. My first thought was going all summer without seeing her again. I felt sick.

I inquired at the nurses station. The nurse on duty told me she had been reassigned to a regular room on the second floor, room number 224. Thank God. I found my way there and stopped outside the door. I leaned into the doorway and peeked inside. She was sitting in the chair with her eyes closed. I panicked. I turned around, went back downstairs and went out the front door. I needed air. I didn't have a clue what to say to her. I saw a large planter on each side of the entrance that had flowers in them. I picked one and quickly returned to her room. I crept in and placed the flower under her nose. Her eyes popped open.

"Mars!"

"The one and only."

She looked really tired.

"So, how are you?" I asked.

"I have been busy all day with tests. I feel like a pincushion. I think they must have taken a gallon of blood from me…not to mention all of the x-rays."

"Wow," I said, as I glanced around the room noticing the lack of mechanical wizardry. I took it as a good sign. "So, when is your doctor going to tell you something?"

"I should have all of the results by Friday afternoon. I'm leaving first thing Friday morning."

She twirled the flower in her fingers and then sniffed it.

"So, who is Venus?"

She wasn't wasting any time, so I came right out with it.

"Venus is the name that I called you in front of my friends at school."

"Why Venus?"

"C'mon Lana, you're not making this easy for me."

"Why Venus, Patrick?"

What did I have to lose?

"As I'm sure you know, the name comes from the Greek goddess. I think you are, without a doubt, the most attractive girl in school."

She called my bluff and I let her have it. She turned crimson. A silence fell over the room. Suddenly, I felt like I had bit off a little more than I could chew. I was trying to think of something else to say when she broke the silence.

"I bet you say that to all of the girls."

She got up, put the flower in a drinking cup and added some water. I was watching her every move.

"What girls?"

"So, you're not dating anyone? I mean, in between all of the drugs that you do."

"What is it with you and all of the references to drugs?"

"I can't figure you out is all. I just don't understand why you would want to throw your life away and seem so nonchalant about it."

I just stood there and looked at her not knowing what to say. I usually had a million answers when my parents asked me the same question. The truth of the matter was I had no clue what was really going on inside of me. I looked down to the floor.

"Well?" She said, crossing her arms.

"I don't know what to say Lana. As far as dating anyone, the answer is no. What about you?"

"Relax Patrick, I'll take it easy on you for now. No, I am not seeing anyone right now either. Here have a seat."

She motioned to the extra chair in the corner of the room. She turned her chair toward mine and sat back down. She started to twirl her hair. I sat down, relieved that she had let me off the hook.

"I have been so busy with my music, school, and activities. I'm very shy to be honest with you."

"There must be a hundred guys that have asked you out."

I wasn't sure if I was asking her or telling her.

"I think most guys are afraid to talk to me. You would be surprised how many boys in school think I'm unapproachable. I'm always with my friends."

I thought about that. It made perfect sense.

"So, how come you never talk to me in school?" She asked.

"Lana we are from two totally different worlds."

"You mean planets...I'm Venus and you're Mars," she said smiling.

"Your friends would have had a field day if I approached you and started chatting you up," I said.

"And what about your friends? What would they say if we were on speaking terms?" She asked.

"Oh, I would be a hero."

"Why is that?"

"You're the best looking girl in the school."

Touché. She went red again. She looked over to the flower on the bedside table.

"Patrick, the flower was so nice of you. You are so much different in person than I imagined...and in other ways, you are just as I thought you might be."

She put her head back in the chair and massaged her temples.

"Is something wrong?" I asked.

"It's these tests. I just don't feel right about any of it. I feel a nice headache coming on right now."

"It does seem like a lot of testing and observation," I offered.

"That's what's bothering me. I feel like someone's not telling me the truth about everything."

"I'm sure that your parents and the doctor are just really concerned about you…they need to find out what's causing the headaches is all."

"I guess so. Tell me Patrick, why are you here at the hospital?"

"Community service," I said, looking away.

"For what?"

"Nothing really."

"C'mon Patrick…everyone in school knows what you're up to. Doing drugs, dealing drugs, robbing houses and God knows what else. People talk you know."

That's the thing about doing drugs. They trick you. When you're using them, everything is fine and dandy. It's all about the ritual, the stigma, and the bad boy reputation. You think you really have it going on. The truth is you can't look at yourself in the mirror. Deep down inside you know something is terribly wrong. You try to stay high, so you don't ever have to see the real you.

This was certainly not the person I wanted Lana to know. Still, I was gloating inside like some sort of rebel with a touch of class. Yeah, I was cool all right. I was a puppet and drugs were running the show. I had no clue what was in store for me. Not an inkling. I sat there looking down at the floor hoping she would change the subject. Did I really expect her not to mention anything about my bad reputation? I was deep in thought.

"Why do you do it Patrick?" She finally broke the silence.

"What?" I said, trying to avoid the question. "Can we talk about this later, I've got to get down to the kitchen…I'm late."

"I'm not letting you off the hook Patrick."

"What makes you think I'm trying to get off the hook?"

"This hospital is full of sick and dying people. Most of them would give anything to trade places with you…to have a second chance at life. You seem so complacent about watching your life go down the drain."

She stood up and went over to the bedside table, picked up her book, and returned to the chair.

"I would see you in school and I always wondered about you. What time are you finished tonight?"

"Nine o'clock," I said, looking at the floor.

I must have been a nice shade of red myself. I got up out of the chair.

"If you want to see me, come by then and we can talk some more."

"Sure Lana, but there's not much to tell."

"I'll be the judge of that. I'll see you later."

She opened up the book and started to read. I didn't know what else to say, so I turned and started to walk out. I stopped at the door. I took one more glance at her. She was really something.

"Goodbye Lana."

"Goodbye Mars."

Her eyes never left the book. I really did not want to think about any of it, so I rushed outside to get high again before work. I was late. No sooner did I get downstairs to the kitchen they were getting ready to collect the dinner trays. John was still showing me the ropes. After his lecture on punctuality, we had about ten minutes before we went upstairs. It occurred to me that I would be face to face with Lana again. I needed some time to collect myself. When we finally arrived on Lana's floor, I went to the far end of the hall with John. He was going to work one side; I was going to work the other. Lana looked out of her doorway and spotted me. She started to walk down the hallway toward me.

"What, you can't even stop in and say hi?"

"I was going to...we started at this end of the hall."

"Now you're avoiding me. That's okay, I can take a hint."

John put the tray he collected on the cart and whispered,

"What is it with you two?"

"Never mind," I said in a hushed tone.

I turned to face Lana again. She was making her way back to her room.

"I'll be down there in a minute," I said loud enough for her to hear me.

"Hey Mars, if you don't want to see me just say so," she said aloud, as she ducked back into her room.

I collected one more tray, put it on the cart, and headed directly to her room. As I entered her room, she took another picture of me.

"Cool it with the camera will you?"

"I'm thinking of making a special section in our senior yearbook featuring you. You should have stopped in here first. A few more pictures and I'll have enough to blackmail you for all of our senior year."

"My boss is out there and you come out yelling down the hallway to me?"

"What are they going to do, fire you?"

She had a point.

"I'll see you at nine. Now let me get back to work."

"Oh, big bad wolf's afraid of little old bossy boss," she teased.

I just shook my head at her and turned to leave.

"Excuse me, Bernard?" She said, as if she was an aristocrat talking to the hired help.

I stopped at the doorway.

"Are you going to take my tray or what Bernard? When you're done with that, please bring me up a bottle of champagne from the cellar."

"Let's go Mr. Fisher, the trays are not going to collect themselves," John said, as he approached Lana's room with the cart.

I turned around to face Lana.

"Bernard, you really should have a talk with the cooks. This meal was atrocious. I wouldn't have served it to the family dog."

"Who the hell is Bernard? You're really going to get me thrown out of here!"

"Oh poor baby! By the way, that apron looks marvelous on you."

She started laughing. I grabbed her tray and hurried out of the room.

"I'll see you at nine Bernard, and don't forget my champagne!"

"Visiting hours end at nine," John whispered to me, as I placed her tray on the cart.

Not for me they don't, I thought to myself. When all the trays were picked up, we brought them downstairs to be washed. I decided while running the dishwasher I would be as honest with Lana as I could about everything. I wasn't looking forward to any more of her interrogation, however, I wanted to spend time with her more than anything in the world. Even though she wasn't the slightest bit impressed with me, things seemed to be going rather well.

Lana wasn't the first person that wanted to know why I wanted to ruin my life with drugs and destructive behavior. My family and local law enforcement had been trying to get me to answer this question for years. My parents were already white knuckling it, hoping I would ask for help before it killed me. Now Lana wanted answers. I would give them to her. I just didn't think I would change…or so I thought.

At a little after nine, I returned to her room and a few people were coming out of her door as I was heading down the hall. It looked like it might be her family. I paused at the water cooler and let them get on the elevator. When I arrived at her room, Lana was sitting in the chair with her eyes closed. I stood in the doorway and just looked at her. All of the sudden I felt uneasy. I went further down the hall and found the bathroom. The vile of cocaine had a small spoon attached to the cap. A five second fix we called it. My friends and me prided ourselves on our drug paraphernalia. When I returned to Lana's door her eyes were open.

"Hi Mars."

"Hi Venus."

"Are you finished for the night?"

"Yep."

"Good, come in and sit down."

She pulled the extra chair closer to hers and patted the seat.

"What time are you being picked up?"

"Ten o'clock," I said, as I sat down. "My dad is coming."

"Good, we have almost a full hour together."

She seemed really happy about spending time with me. At least that is what the cocaine was telling me.

"Was that your family that just left?"

"My parents and my brother. I'm the youngest by three years. Do you have any brothers or sisters?"

"One older brother, one younger sister. My brother graduated last year."

"So did mine. Hey, I wonder if they know each other."

"Probably."

"What do your brother and sister think of all this mess that you're in?"

Oh boy. Here we go.

"They don't approve of it."

"Well, I've been thinking…I'm going to be honest with you. I don't approve of it either. Not one bit."

She crossed her arms and straightened up in her chair.

"You should take things a little more serious. Have you seen the people in this hospital? You're so lucky."

"I hadn't really thought about it."

"Well you should. Don't take life for granted. You never know what tomorrow could bring you. One day you're fine and the next day you're down for the count."

This is what I was afraid of. I didn't know what to say to her. I just sat there and looked at her.

"I guess I can see your point," I managed.

"Next time you're collecting trays, take a really good look at the people you're collecting them from and then count your lucky stars."

We sat and looked into each other's eyes. It seemed like all space and time had stopped. I looked away first.

"Speaking of collecting trays…what was that mess they tried to serve me for dinner?"

"Chicken au Gratin."

"Chicken all Rotten is more like it. There were feathers mixed in with it. I swear. Do you eat the food here?"

"I try not to. You should try washing it off the trays."

"No thanks…I'm starved. Oh Bernard, would you be a doll and run down to the cafeteria and buy me some fruit and a soda?"

"Who's Bernard?"

"My butler."

"You have a butler?"

"I do now."

"Oh great."

"Hey, if you don't want the job I can find someone else to do it."

She looked away and turned her nose up to the air.

"I'll do it…but the cafeteria's closed right now."

"Then get it from the vending machines. Hmm let's see…chocolate and some chips. That's what I want."

"What kind of chips?"

"Bernard, use your head for something besides a hat rack will you? You're supposed to know these things."

"Okay, I'll decide," I said.

"I swear, you can't find good help these days," she teased.

"Sorry your majesty. I'll get right on it."

I stood up and looked at her. This girl was gorgeous, and she had one hell of a sense of humor.

"Bernard, the proper term is get right *to* it. Get right *on* it sounds like you're getting ready to climb on a bicycle."

"Sorry Miss. Anything else?"

"By the time you get me my food Bernard, I'll be nothing but skin and bones."

"I'll get right *to* it."

I left her room and hurried down to the vending machines. I bought her a Hershey bar and some potato chips. I also stole her an apple from the fruit bowl in the cafeteria. I snuck by the nurses desk and returned to her room. I sat back in the chair across from her. I handed her the snacks and the apple.

"Your dinner, Miss."

"I thought you might never make it back. Hey, where's my soda?"

"Downstairs in the vending machine. I forgot it."

"What do you expect me to wash this all down with?"

"Oh, I don't know. There's some water right there in the pitcher by the bed. Try that."

"Well I never. Sassing me will get you nowhere when performance reviews come around Bernard."

She opened up the candy bar and took a bite. Then she started on the chips. She looked me over for a little bit.

"Who would have ever thought I would be sitting here having dinner with Patrick Fisher. If my friends could see me now."

"I'm sure you have enough pictures to collaborate your story."

"I can't wait to get these new ones developed."

"Throw mine in the garbage will you?"

"No way. I finally got some of you for the yearbook."

"You wouldn't."

"Watch me. I have one of you in the hallway at school, but it looks like you're in the middle of a drug deal."

"Are you serious?"

"As a heart attack. Oh Bernard, would you pour me some water please?"

I got up and poured her a drink from the bedside table. I handed her the water and sat back down. She took a few sips.

"It's a great shot," she continued, with a mouth full of chips. "You're standing by the lockers in the hallway with some other wasteoid. Money is changing hands. It would have made the yearbook, but I didn't want to get you in trouble."

"How do you know it was a drug deal?"

"Oh c'mon Patrick. You should just put up a stand and peddle your wares. It's so obvious."

"I didn't realize."

"How could you? You're out of your mind all day long at school. Even someone like me hears the rumors about what you guys are selling or using and for how much."

"I had no idea."

"A word to the wise. It's time to knock off this nonsense. They are probably watching you very close. The police station is right across the street you know."

"I'll keep my eyes open from now on."

"Why not just walk away from everything and start over fresh?"

"I never gave much thought to it."

"It seems like an awful shame to me. A waste of a perfectly good life."

"Can we talk about something else?"

"Absolutely not. Now that I've got you here I want to find out what makes someone like you tick."

"Wonderful."

I needed more cocaine. If I was going to sit through all of this, I wasn't going to take it lying down. I got up out of my chair.

"I'll be right back."

"You're kidding right?"

"I'm just going down the hall to use the bathroom. I'll be right back."

"I'm not done with you yet young man."

"I'm looking forward to it, Miss Steinberg."

"Who's Miss Steinberg?"

"My shrink."

"You see a therapist?"

"I do now, I've got you don't I?"

"Very funny."

"If I'm Bernard the butler, then you're Miss Steinberg the shrink."

I returned to the bathroom and finished the white powder in the vile. It was like a rocket ride straight to the moon. I returned to her room and poked my head in her doorway.

"Excuse me Doc, can we finish my session now?"

"Nope, we're all out of time. We can pick up where we left off on your next appointment."

"Saved by the bell," I said, looking at the clock.

"Hardly. I'll be here all day tomorrow as well."

"Lucky me."

"Your father is probably waiting for you. Will you stop in and see me tomorrow?"

"How much is all of this costing me?"

"For you it's on the house. You're one of my special needs cases."

"Oh, thank you so much!"

"My pleasure."

"Well, I better not keep my dad waiting. I'll see you tomorrow. I'll stop in before my shift starts. Goodnight Venus."

"Goodnight Mars."

I tipped her an imaginary cap and I was off down the hallway. I was in such a good mood I even said farewell to the nurses sitting at the station. They didn't seem to mind me being up there after visiting hours. On the way home, I was thinking about some of the things Lana was trying to get through to me. I wasn't stupid. I knew exactly where she was coming from. Did I really think she would overlook my bad character and start talking to me about the weather? I was blindsided by her. Now I wish she saw me in a different light. She would chew me up and spit me out like a stale piece of gum. Sometimes I can be such a schmuck. I didn't get high again that night.

The next day my mother was late getting home from work. I called the hospital and let them know I would be late. I decided to take a slice of my mother's lasagna with me to work for Lana. I brought a fork and some napkins. When my mother dropped me off, I hurried up to Lana's floor. I asked the nurses if I could use the microwave in the break room to heat up some food. While the food was heating up, I made a quick pit stop in the bathroom for a pick me up. I returned to the break room, put the container of food inside my paper bag and headed off down the hallway toward Lana's room. I could see that the other patients were just starting to eat, so I knew it would be a little while until we picked up the trays. Perfect timing. As I entered her room, she was sitting up on top of the bed with the meal tray on the table next to her.

"Hello Miss Meyers, I'm Dr. Killpatient."

I approached her and extended my hand. She shook it with a big smile on her face.

"They tell me you've been experiencing some headaches. Hmm...Let me see."

I put my hand to her head.

"You don't feel warm. Open up and say ahh."

She humored me and obliged.

"Oh my. That's one hell of a trap door you have there. Perhaps it's the food. What is on the menu tonight?

"Beef Hellington," she said.

"I see. You haven't touched it."

I picked up the tray and set it over on the chair. I put my bag on the table. Lana watched my every move with amusement.

"I have just the thing for you. Just what the doctor ordered," I said, opening the bag. "Homemade lasagna and a cold ginger ale."

"Oh Mars, you didn't."

"The name is Killpatient. Dr. Killpatient, if you please."

I took everything out of the bag and adjusted the table, so it was in front of her over the bed. I put a napkin on her lap and then opened the container of food. I cut a small piece, picked it up with the fork and sat down on the bed next to her.

"Open wide."

"You're going to feed me?"

"Doctor's orders."

She took the food into her mouth and slowly chewed.

"That's delicious."

"See…you're feeling better already."

I put another forkful into her mouth. I poured some ginger ale into one of the drinking cups that were on the table. I put it to her lips and she sipped from it. I wiped her mouth with a fresh napkin. While she was chewing her food, we were looking into each other's eyes. While I was feeding her, it occurred to me that I was stark raving mad for her. I wondered what was going through her mind. We continued like that without saying a word until the container was empty. I put the napkin to her mouth one last time.

"Do me a favor will you Miss Meyers?"

"Anything."

"Please don't let anyone know about this. I could lose my license to practice."

"Not a word," she said, as she zipped her mouth closed, locked it, and threw away the imaginary key.

"Oh, and another thing Miss Meyers," I said, putting everything in the paper bag.

"Yes doctor?"

"That new kid who's doing his community service work here at the hospital…Patrick Fisher I think his name is. Be nice to him. Rumor has it that he's crazy about you."

I got up, walked straight out of her room, and went down to the kitchen to get ready for work. In less than a half hour, I would have to see Lana again. What in the world did I just do?

In no time at all, we were ready to collect the trays. It was the moment of truth. Now that she knew how I felt about her, I was vulnerable. Halfway into our rounds we arrived on her floor. John went one way I went the other. I was so nervous my knees were knocking. I barely took two steps forward when Lana popped her head out of her room and spotted me.

"Excuse me, Dr. Killpatient," she yelled down the hallway, waving her hands wildly.

I hurried over to her and played along.

"Yes Miss Meyers, what can I do for you?"

"Give this note to Patrick Fisher for me and take my tray please."

I took the note from her and entered her room to collect the tray. On my way out I said, "I'll get this right to him." She smiled and watched while me and John picked up all of the trays on the floor and disappeared into the elevator. The note was written in pen on one of the napkins I had brought earlier. It said: I am warming up to you too.

I almost fell over in the elevator. When we saw each other later that evening everything went smooth as silk. For a change, we talked about music, sports, and our families. She never asked one question about drugs or the trouble I was in. For almost an hour, we sat and got to know each other. When I left the hospital that evening, I thought I might actually have a chance with her. I was so exhilarated when I arrived at home that I wanted to call her room number. I thought better of it and was awake in bed for most of the night thinking about her.

I spent the whole next day daydreaming about Lana. I knew that she was going home Friday morning and that she would be hearing from her doctor the same afternoon. I wondered how all of the test results would come out and if they could find a solution to her headaches. It would be the last night I would be seeing her at the hospital. The telephone interrupted my musing. It was my mother. She was asked to work a double shift, so my father would be taking me to the hospital. I would be late again, so I called the hospital and let them know.

By the time my father dropped me off I was so late I went straight to the kitchen. The trays had already been collected. John informed me that "my girlfriend" was looking for me. I started up the dishwasher and began to empty the trays into the garbage. They had served Seafood Newburg. It looked like someone threw up onto a biscuit. Lana must be hungry. When I finished, I bought her some fruit, a nice salad, and a ginger ale. I stopped out front and picked her another flower. I made it to her room by nine fifteen. She was sitting in the chair with her eyes closed. She had the empty chair pulled close to hers. I walked in and plopped myself down in front of her. She opened her eyes.

"Mars!"

"The one and only."

"I didn't think you were coming…and you brought me something to eat. How did you know I was hungry?"

"I saw what they were serving," I said, handing her the salad and soda.

"Good thinking," she said, as she opened the salad.

I went over to the bedside table and set the fruit down. I pulled the flower out of my shirtsleeve and turned around.

"This is for you also."

I handed her the flower. I watched her breath it in. The flower paled compared to her. She wanted to keep the flowers together, so I handed her the cup that she had put the first one into. She dropped it into the cup next to the other one and set them on the armrest of her chair. I sat back down and watched her finish her salad.

"Thank you for the flower and dinner. You're so sweet."

"You're welcome."

"So tell me, how come you don't have a girlfriend? I mean you're so thoughtful and easy to get along with. The image that everyone has of you at school isn't really what your personality reflects."

"Truthfully, I guess it's because I want a really nice girl...not someone who is as messed up as I am."

"I see what you mean," she said, looking at the flowers again.

"I mean come on, how does a guy like me approach a really nice girl anyway? I would be turned down and that would be the end of it. Why bother?"

"To be honest with you, I haven't had much luck with talking to boys and going out on dates or that sort of thing either," she said.

"You're kidding, right?"

"Contrary to everyone's belief, I'm not Miss popularity. Where boys are concerned anyway. I'm to busy with my friends, activities, music, and everything else. I'm actually very shy, as I already mentioned."

"I imagined you with an endless line of options," I said.

"No, every time someone asks me out, I tell them I'm too busy. I guess I'm just not ready yet."

"I see you in the hallways with lots of guys though."

"They're all just friends. I have a ton of guy friends…just nobody that I am romantically attached to is all."

"I never would have guessed."

"Hey Mars, I was thinking that perhaps this summer you and I might keep in touch. I'm leaving first thing in the morning you know."

"I'll have to think about that one," I joked.

"You're an arrogant little punk," she said playfully.

"I'm sorry Miss, I would be honored."

"That's more like it. If we don't make some sort of arrangements, we won't hear from each other until school starts. Is that what you want?"

She was right. She had me. That is exactly how this would have ended up if she hadn't said something to me. I would have let the opportunity slip right through my fingers…then I would have told myself that it's not what I wanted anyway. I would tell myself that she didn't like me anyhow. Drugs were great for that too…justifying missed opportunities. Even so, I needed more cocaine.

"I'll be right back," I said, starting to get out of the chair.

"You're kidding right? Oh no you don't. Park your butt right back in that chair Mister. You're going to get high aren't you?"

"I was thinking about it."

"Let me have it. Give me the drugs Patrick or I will never speak to you again."

I produced a small vile from my pocket and handed it to her.

"What's this?" She said, looking at the dark brown vile.

"Cocaine."

"Wonderful. You won't be needing this anymore."

She stood up and went to her bathroom. I heard the toilet flush.

"You know something Patrick?" She said, marching out of the bathroom.

"What?" I said, slouching down in the chair a little.

She stopped in front of me with her hands on her hips.

"If we are going to stay in contact with each other, you really need to get your act together. Can you do that? I really don't approve of this at all."

She waited for an answer. Her eyes burned through me like a hot bolt through butter. I didn't have an answer for her and slouched the rest of the way down in my chair.

"Your father is going to be here soon."

"I know."

She looked out the window. I needed to make the next move. It was now or never.

"Lana I would like nothing more than to be able to keep in touch with you. It would be great if we could spend some time getting to know each other this summer. Here, sit back down."

I was so nervous that I needed to move around the room. She sat down and I stood up. I couldn't look her in the eye, so I moved to one corner of the room and fidgeted with some equipment on the wall.

"Lana, I don't have any answers about how I ended up in such a mess. There are times when I think about it and I am just as confused as everyone else. Seems like everything happened so quickly, I was in over my head before I knew it. Meeting you has definitely got me thinking about things. For the first time in my life, I wished I never got into this whole mess. I'm actually ashamed about who I am."

I turned and faced her again. She was watching my every move. She put her feet up on my chair. I started to pace from one end of the room to the other.

"My family moved here from New York a few years back and I left my close friends behind. That was the summer before high school. For some reason I was terrified about making new friends and fitting in. I fell in with a group of kids and we all were experimenting with booze and drugs that summer. I felt like I fit in and it all just took off from there."

"What were you like before you moved here?"

"Compared to now? An angel. I was into all kinds of sports and activities. I had four really close friends. I never wanted to move here."

"It must have been hard for you to leave all your friends and everything."

"My family moved around every so often on the account of my father being in the military. When I was growing up it never bothered me much. I took this last move really hard."

"I knew there was a different side to you. I kept telling my friends at school that you couldn't be all bad."

"You talked about me in school with your friends?"

"I spent most of the time defending you. "White trash" was the phrase they used when referring to you."

"Oh really?"

"Well, you didn't exactly try to hide what you were doing Patrick, I mean come on…dealing drugs right in the middle of the school hallways?"

"Good point. I guess I never really cared what anyone else thought about me…until now."

"What am I going to do with you Patrick?"

"Give me your telephone number. Let me take you out this summer. I start work at the William Gregg House next week. We could go there for dinner some night when I'm not working. It would sure beat this hospital food you've been subjected to."

She went over to the bedside table and picked up a pen and a small notepad. She scribbled down something.

"Here's my number. You can call me tomorrow night."

"What should I say if someone else answers the phone?"

"I have a separate line in my room, so don't worry about it."

"What's the extension in this room?"

"Two-twenty four, same as the room number. Why?"

"I'll call when I get home. My dad must be waiting for me."

"That would be great Patrick," she said, as a big smile came across her face.

"Well, I should get downstairs and see if my father is waiting for me."

"Okay, I'll talk to you in a little while," she said.

"As soon as I get home."

Then I did it. I stepped over to her, and gave her a quick peck on the lips as if we were married for fifty years. She didn't seem to object to it, she just stood there. I had the sudden feeling that I overstepped my boundaries, but I wasn't sure. I turned and headed for the door without saying a word. If she objected, she didn't make a sound as I left the room.

When I was down the hall a little ways, a small celebration ensued in front of the nurses station. I looked at the nurses behind the desk, waved the piece of paper in my hand and gave them a couple of steps of my victory dance. Out of the corner of my eye, I saw Lana looking out of her doorway toward me. I turned to face her, tipped my imaginary hat, and took a bow. I spun around and walked into the open elevator. As the doors started to close, I heard Lana laughing. I felt like I was soaring in the clouds and it wasn't because of the drugs. I wasn't even high anymore. Love had sobered me up.

On the ride home, I actually talked with my father. I was feeling different. I hadn't *really* talked to my dad in years. For some reason, it felt like it was time to make some sort of change. When we reached home, I went downstairs and took out my stash of drugs and money. Nothing looked appealing. I had just finished telling Lana I would make a change…then I saw the piece of tin foil. I unfolded the foil and tapped the tiny pills into my hand. LSD. Nine doses. I put it back into its wrapper and placed it on my dresser. I opened the back door and stepped out into the night air.

We had about eight feet of back yard before it dropped down into the brook. I could hear the water babbling over the rocks. The air smelled of moss and damp soil. I went back inside, called the hospital and asked for extension 224.

"Hello?"

"Hi Lana, it's me Patrick."

"Mars!"

"How are you?" I asked.

"I've been reading and waiting for you to call."

"Well, here I am."

"You know something…that was nice…very unexpected, but nice."

"What was?" I said, playing dumb. I wanted to hear her say it.

"That kiss."

"Oh yeah, that. I guess I lost my head. Don't ask me why I did that, I just wanted you to know that I really want to see you this summer."

"What will our friends say?" She asked.

"Nothing if we don't tell them. I think it would be a good idea if we didn't say anything," I said.

"You want to sneak around here and there all summer?"

"I just need some time to get my act together. There's not much to do in town anyway. We can go to the beach. It's also really nice here at my house. We could ride bikes, go for walks, stuff like that."

"We are going to run into someone sooner or later," she said.

"We'll cross that bridge when we come to it. Don't get me wrong; I have no problem being seen with you. I just don't want an uncomfortable situation for you, if we're together and someone sees us."

"I don't care what people think, really Patrick."

"I do…for the sake of your reputation. Everyone knows that I was just arrested for those robberies. Just give me the summer to prove to you that I can do this."

"Do what?"

"You know…change."

"Alright, we'll tip-toe around New Hampshire all summer long. Why don't we wear disguises? I could be Nixon…you could be Spiro Agnew. I have the masks up in the attic somewhere at home," she said.

"Nobody even remembers what Agnew looked like."

"My point exactly. Even in our masks nobody will know who you are."

"Oh you're funny. I just would like some time alone with you without any outside influences," I said.

"I understand. I was just kidding."

"Anyway, guess what I'm going to do as soon as we get off the phone?"

"Come and see me at the hospital?"

"I wish. My parents won't let me use my brother's car until they see some results. I could sneak out the back and ride my bike over?"

"No way. I don't want you to get into any more trouble than you already are."

"Okay, scratch that idea. What I was going to say was that I'm going to throw away all of my drugs as soon as we hang up."

"You're kidding."

"No, I'm dead serious. I am getting rid of everything. A nice sized brook flows right behind our house. I'm going to gather it all up and pitch it out the back door into the water."

"How much stuff do you have?"

"Enough to last me well into the summer."

"I really didn't think you were that bad. When was the last time you were high?"

"I got high tonight, before I came to see you."

"Don't tell me that. I had such a great memory of everything that happened…now it will never be the same."

"I'm sorry, I had no idea it was going to turn out like this between us."

"You seemed fine. How will I ever know if you're using again? What were you on anyway?"

"Cocaine."

"Well, I guess I took care of that. Isn't that expensive?"

"Now you know why I was robbing all of those houses."

"So, how will I know if you're not being honest with me? I mean it Patrick, I won't tolerate it for a minute."

"I'm being honest with you now."

"I guess so, but if I so much as even think you're doing things behind my back…that's it…it's over."

"Fair enough. My mother has been a nurse all her life. Once you meet her, she's going to love you. If there's anything going on, she will let you know…believe me. She tears up my room all the time looking for stuff."

"You poor thing."

"I'm just saying, if there's anything wrong, you'll be the first to know about it."

"I hope so, I'm trusting you Patrick."

"You're not having second thoughts about spending some time with each other are you?"

"No, I just want you to know how serious I am."

"I won't let you down."

"I hope not. Why are you throwing everything in the stream anyway? Why not just put it all in the garbage?"

"This way it will be gone for good. I could always dig it out of the trash if I had second thoughts. I can also tell all of my friends that I am out of everything. They won't be bothering me for long."

"I didn't say you had to get rid of all of your friends."

"I know, but all we do together is use drugs. I would much rather be spending time with you than getting stoned with them."

"That's so sweet. Well, I better be getting to bed if I'm going to get out of here first thing in the morning."

"What are your plans after that?"

"My family's coming to get me at nine, then we're going out for a nice breakfast. I have an appointment to see my doctor at one, to see what the results are from all of the tests they did. You've got to work here tomorrow...right?"

"Yeah, they have me training from 5 to 9 all week. Then I have the weekend off. After that, I work on just Saturdays and Sundays until school starts up again. I start working at the restaurant a few nights a week starting next week as well."

"And you were planning on squeezing me in where?"

"I'll find time for you don't worry."

"I was just kidding. Call me as soon as you get home tomorrow night."

"Sure thing. I hope everything goes well tomorrow."

"Thanks…and Mars?"

"Yes?"

"Thank you for the flowers and the kiss and all you've done for me while I was here. I'll talk to you tomorrow night."

"The pleasure was all mine. Goodnight."

"Goodnight."

I hung up the phone and looked over on the bed. I still had to collect all of the rest of the stuff I had hidden around my room. When I was finished, I put everything on the bed with the drugs and the money. There were enough drugs to take down a small country. Then there was all of the paraphernalia. There were more contraptions than on a surgeon's operating tray. I picked up the whole mess, put it all in a paper bag, and started to go outside.

One of our cats, Frisky, met me at the door meowing to get in. I let him in and stepped out into the cool summer night. It was a nice evening with the moon high in the sky. Some clouds were traveling in front of the moon's light. I walked over to the end of the backyard where it drops down into the water. I turned around and looked up to the living room window. The lights were still on. My father must still be up watching the television. I turned back to the water and began to throw items into the stream. In a couple of minutes, the bag was empty. I had done it.

I wanted to call Lana back and tell her the news. I missed her so much already you would have thought I hadn't talked to her in months. I stood there and looked at the moon and stars in the night sky. Something moved off to my right and startled me. There were all types of animals that lived near the brook. I decided to go back inside incase it was a skunk. I stepped back inside and looked at the clock. It was too late to call Lana. I spent the rest of the night lying in bed thinking of all the things I wanted to do with Lana this summer.

I woke up to an empty house. As I was getting dressed, I saw the piece of foil on my dresser. I was in a hurry to call Lana, hoping I could catch her before she left the hospital. I picked up the money off the bedside table and put it inside a record album with the LSD. I would take care of it later. I dialed the hospital and asked for 224.

"Hello?"

"Hello Venus."

"Oh, hello Mars. Do you know I was up most of the night thinking about you?"

"I was up half the night myself. I knew I should have called you."

"Well in the future, if there's ever any doubts, just go ahead and call me. Remember, if you need to talk about what you're going through, I'm here. Did you get rid of everything?"

"Every last item."

"I'm so proud of you. That's a great start."

"It wasn't easy. I've been doing this just about everyday for almost four years now. I must have thrown out over a thousand dollars worth of stuff. My friends are going to be pissed when they find out."

"Your parents let them come over to the house?"

"Not exactly. We sneak out at night and meet each other on our bikes."

"Well, there won't be any more of that, will there Patrick?"

"No, I'll call them up this morning and tell them I'm finished."

"I thought you wanted to keep our friendship a secret for the summer? They're going to want to know why."

"I just went to court for the robberies, some of them have court next week for the same thing. We should all end up with the same sentence…probation, restitution, and community service. If we get caught with each other it's a violation."

"What's probation?"

"Court supervision. I have to report to a probation officer at the courthouse a couple times a month. He will be drug testing me and checking to see that I'm doing the right thing. It doesn't make sense for me to risk hanging out at night anymore. It's the perfect time to get out of the game without looking soft."

"Who cares what they think?"

"That's easy for you to say. You have tons of friends. It's going to be a lonely summer for me without anyone to do things with."

"You've got me, remember? That's all you need right now. We'll worry about your social life when school starts up again."

"Fair enough…I hope we can spend a lot of time getting to know each other. I really like you. I always have. Do you know we live only a little over a mile from each other?"

"Mars, are you stalking me?"

"Oh that's funny. My friends and me looked up your address years ago. I know right where your house is. Maybe I was stalking you."

"Why didn't you ever call me or stop over?"

"And say what?" I said.

"I'm just teasing."

"Could you imagine what would have happened if my friends and me showed up at your house asking for you?"

"I would have had a heart attack."

"And your brother would have probably chased us out of the yard and called the police."

"Probably…Patrick are you really going to give up the drugs and this life of crime? You're not very good at either."

"I'm going to give it my best shot…I promise."

"I was thinking about you all night. I was hoping you would call this morning. I'm willing to give this friendship a chance if you are."

"It will definitely be interesting. How do you feel this morning?"

"I'm excited. I'm exhausted. I feel a headache coming on. Perhaps I can get a few hours sleep before we go to my doctor appointment."

"I hope everything goes well. You know, I had a little something that would have taken away the worst headache, but the fish are enjoying it right about now."

"You're not very funny. Now I know why you call yourself Dr. Killpatient. There are probably dead fish floating in the water all over the place."

"Funny girl. There's one more thing I wanted to tell you before we hang up."

"Yes?"

I wanted so badly to tell her I was falling in love with her. I knew I was. I could feel it running through my veins. Love was something better than drugs as far as I was concerned. The words were on the tip of my tongue. I told myself it was way too soon.

"That was my first kiss you know…I've never even had a girlfriend before."

"Who would go out with you anyway?" She teased.

"You're not making this easy on me. Oh well, I hope you're ready to have the best summer of your life."

"Pretty lofty goals for a guy who thinks a good time is getting stoned and creeping around in other people's houses."

"Will you stop? This is going to be a great summer."

"I'm counting on it," she said.

"Good. Try to rest until your parents get there. I'll call you tonight as soon as I get home."

"Sounds great. Talk to you later Mars."

"Bye Venus."

I hung up the phone and looked at myself in the mirror. "Yes!" I screamed aloud. I opened up the back door to let some fresh air in. I thought about last night, went outside, and looked down into the water. Nothing was left in sight. It was just as well. I went back inside and prepared to call my friends to let them know I wasn't going to be up to my old tricks. It just didn't make sense anymore. I had something better to do.

My mother called to check up on me around lunchtime. I felt so good I decided to tell her about Lana and my resolve to try to turn my life around. She sounded interested, but somewhat skeptical. The conversation turned into the fact that she didn't understand how I got myself into this whole mess in the first place.

My mother had been a nurse all of her life, but she didn't know much about addiction. Perhaps she was in denial that her son was a drug addict and a thief. These last few years had been especially hard on her. I would have to work on talking to my parents again. I needed to open up the lines of communication. I guess the drugs had taken that away as well. I was going to have to learn to go easy on my parents. They earned the right to be angry with me. They heard this song and dance before, the boy who cried wolf. This time, however, it felt like I meant it.

Morning turned into afternoon and I dialed Lana's number. There was no answer. I called again before my mother drove me to the hospital. Still there was no one home. Afternoon turned into night. I called on my break time. Nothing. I felt uncomfortable. I was worried and insecure at the same time. My thoughts ran from one extreme to the other. I felt like getting high. I had lost the ability to manage my emotions. I could not deal with the feelings, I was too used to numbing everything. I was a wreck. I was more worried about Lana having a change of heart than if she was feeling better. Several scenarios ran through my mind. She was finished with me. Someone had talked some sense into her. I didn't deserve her. The more I thought about it the worse I felt. I would call when I finished work. I would be home soon enough.

I tried her number again as soon as I walked in the door. Nobody answered. I never once thought she might still be with her family or sleeping. I was an emotional mess, but I was sober. I couldn't help feeling it was over between us. I pictured her turning the ringer off on her phone and forgetting she ever met me. This sucks. I watched the television until the eleven o'clock news was over and then I dialed her number again.

"Hello?"

I knew something didn't sound right.

"It's me Patrick."

"Oh hi."

"Lana what's the matter? You sound really sad."

"I don't even know how to tell you this…"

She started to cry.

"Is everything okay?"

"No," she managed, in between sobs.

"Lana just tell me…it's alright."

I was so full of raw emotion I would have sworn she was going to tell me that we were finished. Our relationship was going to be over before it ever started. Stupid me threw everything into the damn brook. How was I ever going to deal with this? I never expected what came out next.

"Patrick there is a tumor inside of my brain. They think I have some type of brain cancer."

"What?"

Now I was really in shock.

"Brain cancer."

She said it again. I heard it the first time.

"That's impossible. You're too young."

"I've been crying all night."

"Are they sure?"

"That's what everything is pointing to. I have a growth in a section of my brain stem that was not noticed last time I had some of these tests done. Oh Patrick, what am I going to do?"

"Everything's going to be alright Lana. I miss you so much."

"Me too," she sniffed.

"Lana are you going to be up for a little while?"

"I don't think I can sleep. Why?"

"I need to see you. Can I ride my bike over? I can be there in ten minutes."

"Sure Patrick, I'll go out and sit on the front porch in a little while."

"I'll see you in a few minutes."

"Okay bye."

I snuck out the back door and walked over to the shed where my bike was. Quietly as possible, I walked it up to the top of the driveway and took off. I found her house easy enough in the dark. I had gone by it on my bicycle hundreds of times. I could see her sitting on the front steps when I coasted up to her driveway. I left my bike at the mailbox and walked up the driveway. I sat down next to her. I put my arm around her.

"Want to go for a walk?"

"Sure. Let me go tell my brother."

She went back inside for a minute. When she returned I opened the screen door for her and took her hand. We interlocked fingers and started walking down the driveway.

"So, what happens now?"

"I have to go to a specialist. We're flying out first thing in the morning. My doctor has made arraignments with a place called the Mayo Clinic, somewhere in Minnesota."

I had a lump in my throat the size of a grapefruit. We walked down the street a little and stopped at the first streetlight. We were out of view from her house. In the soft light she looked amazing, despite the fact that her eyes were puffy from all of the crying she had done. I put my hands on her waist and pulled her close to me. I kissed her on the forehead. I began to slowly kiss her all over her face working my way down to her mouth. She never said a word. When our lips met each other's it was magic…our mouths parted slightly and our tongues began to search each other out.

She put her arms around me and I pulled her tightly against me. Years of wanting and waiting for this moment poured out into that first kiss. We attached ourselves to each other for a while, stopping only to give each other a peck on the lips in between hot wet kisses. It was just how I dreamed it would be. We separated and looked at each other in the light. We looked at each other as if we might never see one another again. There was passion tempered with fear in her eyes.

I will never forget that long moment of silence as we just stood there looking at each other. Both of our eyes welled up with tears. I looked to the ground as tears fell off my cheeks. I looked back to her face again and whispered into her ear.

"I bet they're wrong. I want to be with you no matter what."

"Oh Patrick, I'm so glad I met you."

She started crying again. We put our arms around each other and just stood there on the side of the road and wept. A car drove by and we did not move an inch. I was crying for her. I was crying out everything I had bottled up over the years with the drugs. She looked into my eyes when we both had stopped.

"I want to be with you too," she managed.

Our faces were wet with tears. We wiped each other's faces and calmed each other down. We belonged to each other. The rest of the world was far away.

"Let's get you back home, so you can get some rest. You have a long trip tomorrow."

"I don't think I'm going to sleep a wink. Don't leave me just yet."

She squeezed my hand tightly. We walked back to her house and sat down on the front steps. She rested her head on my shoulder.

"What if your brother or parents come to the door looking for you?"

"I already told them I met someone from school. They're going to find us out sooner or later."

"Later would be better."

"You're such a little chicken shit."

"Hey, you just kissed me with that mouth."

"I'm sure you've heard worse."

"I had my first full day today without getting high," I whispered.

" I was going to ask you how you were doing. Was it hard?"

"Only when I couldn't get a hold of you on the phone. To be honest with you, I thought we were finished.

"Finished? We haven't even started," she laughed.

"I know. Without the drugs, I have been a little on edge with my feelings and emotions. Everything seems to be messed up. Either I'm not feeling anything or I'm a nervous wreck…there's no in between."

"You didn't think it was going to be easy did you?"

"I hadn't really thought about it."

"You'll be fine. Whatever you do, don't get high. Everything will eventually fall into place."

"I hope so. I'm like a cat on a hot tin roof right now."

"In a few months you'll look back on all of this and be glad that you did it. Trust me."

"I hope so. Hey, I told my mother about you."

"Really? Do you think she will like me?"

"Are you kidding? She is going to love you. I will introduce you to my family when you get back home. When will you be back?"

"We're not sure. However long it takes to successfully diagnose me and recommend a treatment plan. My doctor tells us it is one of the best facilities in the country. I couldn't be in better hands."

"Lana is everything okay? Are you alright?" A voice said from behind us.

Her parents were at the screen door.

"Yes Mom, I'm fine. This is Patrick, the boy in my class that I met at the hospital. He rode his bike over to be with me."

"Hello Patrick, that was nice of you," her mother said.

"Hello Mr. and Mrs. Meyers. I figured she might need someone to talk to. I live just over on Beaver Brook…it was no trouble getting here."

"Well honey, we're going to bed now. We have an early flight. You should try and get some rest," her father said.

"I will Dad, just a little while longer."

"Sure thing honey. Nice meeting you Patrick."

"Goodnight Mr. and Mrs. Meyers, it was a pleasure meeting you. I wish you a safe trip. Everything's going to work out just fine, I'm sure of it."

"Thank you so much. Goodnight," her mother said.

After they left Lana looked at me and laughed.

"Well, I guess my parents are out of the way. You were so polite. Where did all that come from?"

"I wasn't raised by wolves you know. It's not your parents that I'm worried about; it's your brother who concerns me. What if he tells them about me?"

"He's already been sworn to secrecy. He did say that if you hurt me he's going to kill you though."

"Oh, I feel so much better now. Thanks."

"What? Are you planning on breaking my heart?"

"I wouldn't think of it."

"Then you have nothing to worry about."

"I am worried about you though."

"I'm going to be fine. My doctor gave me something to help with the headaches until I get to the specialists. He says they are the best in the country at what they do. I'll be back in your arms in no time."

I kissed her on the cheek. I figured the best way to keep her mind off things was to make plans for the future…our summer together. We ended up talking until the early morning hours. When we were finished, we had a whole list of things we wanted to see and do together.

"Well, I should get home before my parents get up for work. They might go downstairs and check up on me."

"You're going to leave little old me all alone?" She said in her southern belle voice.

"Can I come with you?"

"I don't think you would fit into my suitcase. It's a great thought though."

We both stood up on the front porch. I put my arms around her waist and we kissed passionately for a few minutes. Kissing her was like tasting some new exotic fruit for the first time. We couldn't get enough of each other. If there was a Heaven, surely I was standing right next to it.

"That was so nice. Guess what?" She whispered.

"What?"

"You're the first boy I ever kissed like that."

"That makes two of us."

"Really? Who was the first boy you kissed?"

"You're a real comedian. You know what I mean. Wow, I'm going to miss you like crazy."

"Me too."

"Get a pencil and a piece of paper. I'll give you my number. You can call me as soon as you are settled in your room. I'm off all day tomorrow. Once I know your room and the telephone number I can call you from then on."

"I'll be right back."

She disappeared inside. I didn't want this feeling to ever end. I hadn't felt this good in years. I had a completely new outlook on life. Screw my friends. I was turning over a new leaf. She returned with a pencil and some paper. I wrote down my number and gave her a smooch on the lips.

"That's it?" She said.

We fell into another round of kissing. She dropped the paper and pencil, put her hands under my shirt, and rubbed my back. I put my hands in her back pockets. I pulled her as close to me as possible.

"Oh my. Keep that tiger in its cage will you?" She whispered into my ear."

"He's harmless, really. See what you do to me?"

We separated and looked at each other one last time. She started to twirl her hair with her finger.

"Are you going to be okay without me?" She finally said.

"I'll be stark raving mad without you *and* the drugs," I said, stepping off the porch.

"And stay out of other people's houses," she added.

"Very funny. Call me once you're settled in."

"I will. I'm going to try and get a few hours sleep, if not, I'll sleep on the plane."

"Good idea."

"Goodnight Mars," she said, waving the tips of her fingers to me.

"Sweet dreams Venus."

I turned and walked down the driveway. I climbed on my bike and turned to look and she blew me a kiss from the front porch. I blew one back and peddled off down the road. It was a ten-minute ride back to my house. I think I made it home in five. I don't think my wheels ever touched the ground. The air was cool and crisp on my face. I put my bike on the side of the shed, went around to the back door, and entered my room. My parents would be up soon. I fell into bed and was lying there thinking about Lana. She was going off to some fancy hospital. I didn't have a clue how I was going to make it through the next few days. I missed her already. My heart felt like a brick. I had told her parents that everything was going to be all right. What did I know? I wasn't even sure if I was going make it through the weekend without getting high. I actually cried myself to sleep.

I woke up to the ringing of the telephone. My mother called me from her lunch break to check up on me. I was actually glad to hear her voice. I took a few minutes to tell her about Lana and her condition.

"Do you know where they are sending her for diagnosis?" She asked, showing interest.

"The name of the place is the Mayo Clinic."

"Oh good. That's perhaps the best in the country right now. She will be in good hands there. I wouldn't worry about anything until she is looked at. Well, I have to get back to work. I'll see you when I get home."

"Thanks Mom."

My mother knew all about these things. Suddenly I felt a closeness to my mother that had been gone for years. I felt like talking with my mother, but listened as she hung up the phone. In my family love was something shown, not talked about. It was always somewhere just below the surface of things. I knew deep down inside that my parents were doing the very best they could for me.

When my mother arrived home, I was upstairs watching television. We talked while we waited for my father to get home from his overtime shift. My mother started to get dinner ready.

"What did you say her name was? The girl that you met from school?"

"Her name is Lana. I met her while I was collecting trays on my first night of training. She was there for observation and tests because her doctor couldn't figure out what's been causing the headaches she's been getting."

"She's in your class?"

"Lana's one of the smartest in my class. She's into sports and music and she's one of the yearbook photographers."

"She must know about your past then?"

"That's the funny thing. Once we met, we seemed to hit it off rather well during her stay. Before she left, she offered to stay in contact with me over the summer if I felt that I could straighten myself out."

"Sounds like she's got her head on her shoulders."

"We've been talking on the phone a lot. I will introduce you to her as soon as she gets back."

"That would be nice. I just hope you can follow through this time. You have your father and me crazy you know. We have heard this tune before."

"I know Mom. It's over don't worry. I want so badly for things to work out with Lana that I'll do anything."

"What about your troublemaking friends?"

"They're all going to court next week. I've already called them and told them I am all done. I told them you found all kinds of things in my room and threatened to call my probation officer unless I really did something with myself. I'm all through with them."

"Tell them whatever you have to, but I don't want any of them over here. Ever."

"Can Lana come over?"

"Of course. You do seem different this week. How's the community service going anyway?"

"Fine, I'm basically doing one of the dietary aide's positions."

"That's good. Perhaps you can get a regular job there when all of this blows over."

"Anything's possible. Hey, perhaps Lana can come to dinner some night. I brought her some of your lasagna, she loved it."

"She can do whatever she wants if it's going to help you out of this mess."

"Thanks Mom."

I got up off the couch and headed to the basement door. I could feel my mother's eyes on me as she stood in front of the stove. I stopped at the door and faced her.

"Mom, have you ever seen a person my age with cancer?"

"Sure."

"What's it like?"

"It's very sad. It all depends on what type and how serious it is, but let's just wait until the experts look her over. Okay?"

"I will," I said, starting down the stairs.

I felt like crying again. I felt like getting high. I wanted this all to go away. I did not want to feel like this. I thought of Lana. My Venus. I tried to picture her with cancer. I told myself it could never happen to her. With those thoughts, I changed my mind about getting high. It was Lana I really wanted. I was so lucky to have her. Most girls wouldn't give me the time of day. I wasn't about to do anything that would ruin our relationship. No sooner than I sat down to wait for dinner, the phone rang. I picked it up on the first ring.

"Hello?"

"How are you Mars? I miss you so much."

"Venus!"

"Well, we're here. My parents are filling out paperwork and whatever else they have to do. I'm calling from a payphone."

"I'm glad you made it safely. My mother and I were just talking about you. She can't wait to meet you."

"Oh yeah, well I talked about you the whole way here. Well, when I wasn't sleeping. My parents want you to come over for dinner when we get back."

"Your brother's not going to say a word? I'm sure he knows who I am."

"Who are you? Jesse James? C'mon Mars!"

"I'm serious, what if your parents find out about my past?"

"My brother said he's never seen me so happy...even with everything that's going on. He asked me if you had cleaned up your act. I told him yes, I just didn't mention that it was only day number two."

"Good thinking. I feel a little better."

"He did mention breaking your neck if you hurt me again though."

"Wonderful."

"When the time comes, you can tell my parents about your past."

"Not likely. Did you get your room number yet?"

"No. We're going to the cafeteria to get something to eat first. By the time we're finished, they should be ready to admit me. I'll call you tonight."

"Great. We are going to be eating dinner here very shortly, so I'll let you go."

"Oh Mars, I can't wait to get home and take more pictures of you."

"Oh boy. Call me later."

"Okay. Bye Mars."

"Bye."

With my brother away in the Air Force and my sister gone to her summer camp, it was the first dinner alone with my parents since school ended. It seemed like things were getting better as each day went by. My parents could never stay mad at me for long and always gave me the benefit of the doubt until I let them down again. We talked about what I was doing at the hospital and starting my new job at the restaurant next week. My mother and I talked a little bit more about Lana and her condition. When the meal was over it was business as usual. My father retired to his chair with the newspaper and the evening news while my mother cleared the table and did the dishes. I went down to my room to watch my own television or to listen to music. I was in my room for a few hours when the phone rang.

"Hello?"

"Yes, I would like to speak to Dr. Killpatient and don't try putting me through to the answering service again."

"Why this is Dr. Killpatient, may I ask who's calling?"

"Lana Meyers."

"Why hello Miss Meyers. What can I do for you?"

"I need you to make a house call."

"What seems to be the problem?"

"If these doctors here take one more test I'm going to scream. Every time someone comes near me, they have a needle in their hand. I'm tired of being their pin cushion."

"It's all part of the process Miss Meyers."

"What process? Scarring me for life?"

"I'll tell you what…when you get back into town I'll schedule you for an examination right away."

"What kind of examination? Does it involve whipped cream and soft hands?"

"Nope. Feathers and chocolate syrup."

"Sounds messy."

"It is. It's the cleaning up that I look forward to."

"Mars you're a pervert."

"Hey Venus you're the one who called looking for Dr. Feelgood."

"I called Dr. Killpatient."

"Same doctor. He's got a split personality."

"Oh great."

We both laughed.

"Hi baby. I miss you so much. So, tell me how your day went."

"It feels like I went through an exorcism."

"That bad huh? How do you feel?"

"Tired is all. My parents just left. Oh, let me give you my room number and the main number to the switchboard downstairs. Do you have something to write with?"

"Sure, one minute."

I found a pen and paper and took the number down. I told her I would call her right back, so I would be billed for it. I dialed the hospital and asked for room number 117. The operator put me through.

"Hello? Shots for tots. You trick them, we stick them."

"Very funny."

"I thought so."

"So, did they give you an idea of how long you would be there?"

"Well, I know I'm scheduled for tests tomorrow and Monday is all. Once they diagnose me, I guess the plan is to send me somewhere close to home if treatment is needed. If they have to operate or do any procedures I will have them done here."

"At least you're in good hands. My mother also said it is one of the best in the country. Let's keep our fingers crossed."

"I don't know what they gave me, but I haven't had any headaches all night. I'm awful sleepy though."

"When's the best time to call you?"

"Try anytime. Visiting ends at nine and that's when my family leaves. If I'm not in my room, I will be getting tests done. You should see this place. I'm taking lots of pictures."

"Who's collecting your meal trays? I know how you can be with the hired help."

"Mars do I detect possible jealousy?"

"Perhaps."

"Well his name is Gerard. I have him running all over the hospital for me. He brought me dinner tonight and he says, for me, the cafeteria is always open."

"You're kidding right?"

"Nope. He's sweet and sexy. Did I mention that he is much older than I am? Older men are so dreamy."

"Well good. I hope you and him have a great time together."

"He's here right now. He's just waiting for you to hang up the phone, so we can get back to our card game."

"Wonderful."

"Oh Mars stop sulking. I couldn't. I'm your girl."

"I was getting worried."

"Yeah right. A girl named Theresa picked up my tray. You would love her. She makes fun of the food right along with me."

"Well, as soon as you get back my mother said you could come for dinner. She will put some meat back on your bones. I told her you loved her lasagna."

"I can't wait. Well, I should finally try to get a good night sleep. I've got to be up bright and early for the doctors in the morning."

"Okay, I'll call you at some point tomorrow. If you're not in your room I will get a hold of you after nine and we'll catch up then."

"Sounds good. Wish me luck. I will talk to you tomorrow. Goodnight Mars."

"Sweet dreams. Goodnight Venus."

The next couple of days were perhaps the hardest for me. I was going through a multitude of feelings and emotions. I was waiting to hear a complete diagnosis on Lana's condition. I used the short leash that my parents had me on as an excuse to stay away from my friends. I wasn't drinking or using drugs, but that's not to say I hadn't thought about it. Talking to Lana always strengthened my commitment to remain on the right track. We spent hours on the phone each day getting to know each other better. The phone bill was going to be out of this world.

We talked about our families and growing up. Like most people, she wanted to hear about my time in Africa. I learned that her father was in banking and her mother sold real estate. She was born and raised in New Hampshire. Except for a few trips to New York and Boston, she had only been to Florida once on a vacation. She planned on going to the Berkeley School of Music in Boston for her degree in music. I heard in school that she was an excellent piano player. Lana could also play the guitar and flute. She told me she wanted to strengthen her voice and record her own album. Me on the other hand, hadn't given a thought about college or what I wanted to do with my life after high school. Lana really had her act together.

When I wasn't on the phone with Lana, she was always on my mind. I couldn't stop worrying about her or thinking about her coming home. I started my new job at the restaurant and that was going well. During the middle of the week, Lana said she would know something definite by Friday. Time was at a standstill. Time was odd like that. If you were in anticipation of an event in the future, the days crawled by.

If you were living life to the fullest, you couldn't keep track of where the days went.

The key was having enough to do while waiting. I kept as busy as I could, but my thoughts always returned to Lana. It was if I was sleepwalking, or I was running on autopilot. Finally, I woke up and it was Friday morning. I didn't have anything planned except mowing the lawn and waiting for Lana's call. It was shortly before three when the phone rang. It was Lana.

"Hello?"

"Patrick?"

She sounded distant. Serious. She only called me Patrick when she wasn't fooling around. At least that's how it seemed.

"Yes baby, I'm here."

"It's brain stem cancer," she said in a low tone.

She must have been in shock. I went into shock. I couldn't even speak. My stomach knotted up and my hands started to shake. There was a long silence.

"Oh, my God. Baby are you all right? So, what now? When can I see you again?"

There was a longer silence. I could only imagine what she looked like on the other end of the phone.

"Are you sure you still want to?" She said, her voice trailing off.

I could hear her crying.

"Lana no matter what happens, I'm going to be with you. Always. I love you so much."

I said it and I meant it…every word of it.

"Really?"

I tried to brighten her up and stop myself from completely breaking down.

"Lana I'm going to be here for you. Nothing has changed between us. Okay?"

"You're so sweet Patrick."

"So, what happens next? When do you come home?"

"There are a few more tests. They can't operate because of the location of the tumor. It's too dangerous. They are deciding right now on the best treatment for me. If everything goes well, I should be home Monday morning."

"Promise me that you will let me see you as soon as you get home."

"I promise. Right now, I need to get some sleep. My parents are still talking with the doctors. My mom seems to think they made a mistake. She is having a real hard time with all of this. They ended up giving me a sedative to calm me down. It has been the worst day of my life."

"Try to get some rest sweetheart. I will call you tonight after visiting hours are over. Everything is going to be all right. I'm right here by your side…okay? I love you so much."

"Oh Patrick. I love you too."

"There's my girl. Sleep. We'll talk later."

"Bye Patrick."

"Sweet dreams love."

I still had the receiver in my hand and there were tears running down my cheeks. I hung up the phone. It felt like I swallowed a mouthful of sand. My heart seemed like a nail had been pounded into it. I knew I was going to break down and that's exactly what I did. I cried, as I never had before. I cried like the day I was born. My mother would be home soon. I did not want anyone to see me in this condition. I went out the back door and went for a walk. I walked along the brook. The water was very low. There was a spot where I could cross on top of some boulders not far from my house.

There were several large stones close to each other and I made it across easily. I knew there were no houses on this side. I decided to walk along the other side toward my house. There was a shady spot directly across from my house and I sat down on the pine needles. I looked up and down the stream and listened to the cool water flow over the rocks and stones.

My thoughts were consuming me. It felt like someone kicked me right in the gut. I stood up, turned my back to my house and walked straight into the woods. After a short distance, I saw a little clearing up ahead. When I stood in the clearing, I realized that the pine trees formed a perfect circle around me. There was a thick blanket of pine needles on the ground. Not one of the six trees had any branches near the ground, so I was able to move around.

I looked between the trees back toward my house. The foliage was too dense to see the other side of the brook. I could hear the water gently moving along, falling over obstacles. It was a shady spot, hidden from sun that loomed overhead. I thought it would be a nice place to bring Lana. A picnic. I sat down. My eyes began to well up again. Not again I thought. Get up. Keep moving. I would remember this spot. I started for home. I couldn't wait to speak to Lana again. I would have to face my family first though.

When I arrived home, my mother was at the kitchen sink washing a chicken for dinner. She took one look at me and knew something was wrong.

"Mom Lana has brain stem cancer."

"Oh Patrick I'm so sorry. How far along is it? Do they know how they are going to treat it yet?"

"I don't know yet. They just gave her family the news. Mom, what's going to happen to her?"

I knew my mom was one of the best nurses in the country. She had taken care of Sammy Davis Jr. when he had lost his eye. She also cared for Geronimo's only living son, Robert, when he was in the hospital with pneumonia and diabetes. Before he passed, my mother told him of my Native heritage and he made me an honorary member of the Apache tribe. She knew her stuff. It suddenly occurred to me that the type of treatment must have something to do with how far along the cancer was. My mother was looking out the front window into the yard. Perhaps she was reflecting on all of the pain and suffering she had seen over the years. She finally answered me.

"Let's wait until we see how they plan to treat it. There are several excellent cancer units in hospitals nearby. The hospital where you are doing your community service can handle most cases."

She turned to look at me. I suspected she was holding something back from me. I wondered if the doctors and Lana's parents were doing the same. I had to get downstairs before I fell apart again. I had a lot of questions and no answers. I had to find something to keep me busy. I could clean my room. That would burn a few hours. I took some cleaning supplies from under the sink and headed for my room.

"What are you doing?" My mother asked.

"I'm going to clean my room. If I don't keep busy I'll go nuts," I said, opening the door to the basement.

"Patrick?"

"Yes?" I said, stopping on the landing.

"It's going to be alright."

"I know Mom."

I continued down the stairs. I didn't know anything for sure. I felt lousy. That was the only thing I was sure of. I avoided dinner altogether. My mother would explain things to my father. I couldn't face anyone right now. I would have to learn how very soon though. Lana would be coming home. I would go through anything to be with her. I finished tidying up my room and brought the cleaning items back upstairs. My mother was finishing with the dishes and my father was reading the paper with the news on.

"I have your plate on the counter there. Would you like me to heat it up?" My mom offered.

"I'll get it, thanks Mom."

I returned to my room with my dinner. In a couple of hours, I could call her. I managed to eat what little I could of my supper. I couldn't get my mind off Lana. I picked up the phone and dialed the number. When the operator answered, I gave her the extension. The phone was ringing.

"Hello?"

"I just wanted to call and tell you how much I care about you and how much you mean to me. I also wanted to thank you for being my friend. I know your family's there. I will call back later. I miss you so much."

"That's sweet Patrick, but Lana's fast asleep. We are all here around her bed keeping an eye on her. I'll be sure to tell her when she wakes up."

"Mrs. Meyers?"

"The one and only."

"Oh boy. I feel like such a fool."

"For caring about our daughter? Nonsense. She's going to need someone like you around."

"How is she? Have you heard any more news?"

"Well, it's definitely a cancer in the brain stem called a glioma. The severity is determined on a scale from one to four. A stage four glioma is the most serious. As it is right now, because of the location, it's not feasible to operate. We are all praying that the doctors have some good news for us tomorrow as to what stage she is at and a treatment plan."

"Well, I will be praying for her on this end. I would also like to extend my heartfelt condolences to your entire family. I know this must be extremely hard on all of you."

"Thank you so much Patrick. Will you be stopping by for dinner when we return home?"

"First chance I get. Count on it."

"Good. I'll tell Lana you called."

"Mrs. Meyers?"

"Yes?"

"Lana is the nicest girl I have ever met. She is so pretty and talented. I will take good care of her I promise."

"I'm sure you will Patrick. You're all she talks about."

"I'll be there for her no matter what."

"Say your prayers Patrick. My baby needs one of God's miracles right about now."

"I will. I will see you soon. Goodnight."

"Goodnight Patrick."

When I hung up the phone, it hit me like a freight train. Lana was just telling me how you never knew what tomorrow was going to bring you. I realized now how I had been taking everything for granted. As my parents called it, I was having a rude awakening. I was sobering up and it hurt. I needed to talk to my mother. I wanted someone to know how I was feeling. My parents were worried sick about me. How many sleepless nights had they been through on my account? I figured I would come to an understanding with them.

I went upstairs. My mother was in the bedroom folding laundry. My father was still watching television. I was thinking about what I was going to say to her when it occurred to me that I really didn't know how to talk to my mother anymore. Sure we talked, but not about what was going on inside of me. I stood in the kitchen and thought about what I would like to say to her.

You know I have been doing the right thing since I met Lana. Things are different now. I feel like I have a fresh start with her. I know I put you and Dad through a lot. I just need you both to give me a new start here at home as well. It's not easy, but I am giving it my best shot. Okay? That sounded so phony. I walked into her bedroom and just started crying. My mother stopped what she was doing and put her arms around me.

"It will be alright. Everything's going to be alright," she said to me.

"I just feel so bad. Everything that's going on with Lana combined with everything I put you and dad through. I'm a ball of raw emotions. Without the drugs and alcohol it seems that all of my feelings are intensified."

"It's just going to take time Patrick that's all. We did our best to raise you children. I guess me and your father feel like we missed something somewhere."

"Mom, it's nothing that you did or didn't do. It happens all of the time in all types of families. All of my friends come from good homes too. Their parents are going through the same thing as Dad and you."

"What's going on in here?" My father said, standing at the bedroom doorway.

"I think our son is finally starting to grow up."

"For your sake son, I hope so. Life's too short to throw it all down the drain with your foolishness."

My father never spoke truer words.

"Have you heard from Lana?" My mother asked.

"I spoke with her mother a little while ago. It's called a glioma in the brain stem or something like that. It cannot be operated on. They are trying to determine what stage the cancer is at before they recommend a treatment plan. Perhaps they will know more tomorrow."

"Well, let's just hope they caught it early enough," my father said.

"Let me know what's going on when you hear something," my mother said.

"Hang in there son. I'm sure she'll get through this alright," my father said.

"Thanks Dad."

"Here, take these clothes down with you. Are you feeling a little better?" My mother asked.

"I think so."

I took the clothes from my mother and headed back downstairs. My father returned to his television and my mother continued with her laundry. Somehow, things did seem a little bit better. It seemed like we were starting to connect as a family again.

That night Lana and I spoke on the phone until the early morning hours. She thought it was funny that I said all of those sweet things to her mother on the phone. She accused me of making a pass at her mom. We had a few good laughs over that. We were really getting to know each other, but everything was happening over the phone. Lana wanted to come home, diagnosis or no diagnosis. I told her if she received any news before I had to go to the hospital to give me a call, otherwise I would try her at some point during the day.

The next day I took the money out of the record album and headed out on my bike. I rode all the way to the mall in Manchester to get something for Lana. I looked in every jewelry store and finally settled on a solid fourteen karat gold heart shaped locket and a diamond cut rope chain to hang it from. It took most of my money, but then again it really wasn't my money at all. I would give it to her as soon as she came home from the hospital. I would have to get by on the little bit of money I made from the restaurant.

I arrived at home and went downstairs to put the locket in my dresser and get ready for my community service. I kept opening the velvet box and admiring Lana's gift. She was going to love it. The locket opened up, so that you could put two tiny heart shaped pictures inside if you wanted. I had just closed my bureau drawer when the phone rang.

"Hello?"

"Patrick it's me, I wanted to catch you before you went to the hospital."

She called me Patrick, not a good sign.

"How are you sweetheart?"

There was a long silence. I could tell that she had been crying.

"The tumor that I have is very fast growing. The doctors say I am between a stage three and four somewhere. They won't know for sure until they monitor me for a while. It's no wonder that nothing showed up last time I had testing done."

"What about treatment?"

"It's so advanced that the only option is immediate chemotherapy. I can go to the hospital at home for infusions."

"Is that going to stop the cancer from growing or get rid of it?"

"We won't know until I start treatment and they can monitor the tumor. I am getting my first treatment in a few hours. I'm a little worried about the side effects though."

"If it helps you get better then it's worth it right? So, when are you coming home? You would feel better if you were at home."

"I have been telling everyone the same thing. We are leaving first thing Monday morning. I am tired of bad news. I am tired of crying. I just want to go home now."

"When you get home I'm going to spend as much time as possible with you. Every chance I can. We'll get through this together."

"They gave me some more pills to calm me down and help me sleep. You should have seen me a few hours ago… I was a mess."

"Anybody who's been through what you just have would be upset. Get some rest and I'll try you when I get home from the hospital."

"How are you doing Patrick?"

"So far, so good. Worried sick about you…I have been on the straight and narrow since I threw everything away. I have also been talking to my parents a little more. Everything's slowly coming together."

"I knew you could do it."

"I think it's the hardest thing I've ever done. Well, get some rest and I'll call you tonight when I get home."

"Okay."

"Lana none of this has changed how I feel about you. We'll get through this together no matter what it takes."

"You're so sweet. I'll talk to you tonight."

"Bye sweetheart."

"Bye Patrick."

I had no idea how I was going to get through all of this. I knew her condition was serious. This was all happening too fast. I just wanted to know if I was going to lose Lana to cancer. My thoughts were all over the place. My father dropped me off at the hospital and I faired no better there. I was in my own little world just going through the motions. My own troubles seemed small compared to what Lana was going through. I had to remain strong for her. I had to be by her side when she needed me. When I called her later that night, there was no answer. I knew she must be sleeping and was probably taking some medication to help her rest. I would try her first thing in the morning.

When we spoke in the morning, she was very sick from her treatment. The good news was she would be coming home on Monday morning for sure. We decided the best thing for her to do was rest. I would check up on her that night went I was finished at the hospital. I spent most of Sunday worrying about Lana. I felt so badly about what she was going through, that I was more determined than ever to do the right thing. I worked in the garden with my father to keep busy during the day. I updated my parents of Lana's condition over lunch. At work that evening, John even asked how Lana was doing.

I was hurting a lot less than the night before, but I was far from all right. I felt weak, like all the life had been sucked out of me. When my father picked me up at the hospital, he told me that Lana had called with a message for me. She was going to bed early, so she could get out of the hospital on time. She would call me as soon as she arrived home Monday afternoon. When I arrived home, I decided to retire myself. I was exhausted from a combination of worrying about Lana and letting my imagination run away with what may happen to her. I knew when I woke up the next morning I would finally be seeing her at some point during the day. I had my first good night of sleep in over a week.

Lana called me at one-thirty in the afternoon. I wasn't working at the restaurant, so I could spend some quality time with her. I showered and grabbed the locket and headed off on my bike. She was waiting for me on the front steps when I turned into the driveway. She looked amazing. I was so lucky to have her in my life. She really was special.

"Mars!"

She didn't even give me time to put the kickstand down on my ten-speed. We were in each other's arms. I don't think we ever held each other as tightly as we did that moment. She grabbed me by the hand and led me inside. Lana's parents were sitting at the kitchen table.

"Hello Mr. and Mrs. Meyers," I said, giving her father a firm handshake.

"Hello Patrick. It's a hot one out there today isn't it?" Mrs. Meyers said.

"It sure is. I worked up a sweat just riding my bike over here."

"Do you want a glass of lemonade?" Lana asked.

"Sure, if it's not too much trouble."

"No trouble at all."

Lana poured us each a drink and handed me mine.

"Well, we have a lot to catch up on."

She took me by the hand and led me off down the hallway. I turned back toward Lana's parents.

"It was nice seeing you again, but I have to go now. She's the boss."

Her parents laughed. We entered her bedroom and she locked the door behind us.

"What if your parents come?"

"Mars, she smiled. Were you this nervous when you were sneaking around in other peoples houses?"

"Actually, yes."

She kicked off her sneakers and told me to do the same. She went over to the bed and stretched out. Her head was propped up by several large pillows she had against the headboard. She patted the empty side of her bed for me to join her. I went around and lay down next to her. I was so nervous it must have looked like the mob had laid me out in cement.

"Get comfortable, will you?" She said.

She seemed to be in good spirits. There were pictures all around her room on the walls.

"You took all of these?" I said, looking around the room.

"Every last one."

I looked around a little more and then toward the door. She followed my line of sight. She started clucking like a chicken.

"Shhh!" I said.

"Scared to death. You're petrified," she teased.

She started clucking again, this time louder. The more I tried to quiet her down, the louder she clucked. It was a losing proposition.

"Okay. Okay. I'm relaxing," I whispered.

"Nobody's going to bother us. Trust me."

I stretched out next to her, reached into my pocket, and pulled out the velvet box.

"I have something for you."

She sat up and took the box from me. She opened it very slowly.

"Oh my God, it's beautiful. Is this really for me?"

"No, it's for your brother."

She laughed. She took it out of the box and held it up in front of her.

"Nobody has ever given me anything this nice before."

"Try it on."

"Okay, help me."

She handed me the locket and turned her back to me. I sat up, put it around her neck, and fixed the clasp. She jumped up and looked in the mirror on the back of her door.

"Patrick it's so nice. Thank you."

"You're welcome."

She came back over to the bed and stretched out next to me. We fell into a kiss. We kissed for a long while searching for the rhythm we had perfected before she left. She whispered into my ear.

"Take off your shirt."

I silently obliged. She ran her fingers down my chest and stopped at my belly, making circular motions with the tips of her fingers. She continued downward and gently ran her hand across the front of my jeans. She couldn't help but feel the swelling in my loins.

"Looks like the tiger is out of his cage."

"He roams around from time to time."

I reached for the buttons on her shirt and began to undo them. She didn't stop me. When I finished, she sat up, removed her shirt, unhooked her bra, and let it fall to the bed. She was half naked in front of me. She lay back down next to me and we took turns exploring each other in between long passionate kisses. I was dizzy with passion. We separated for a moment and were lying on our backs looking up to the ceiling.

"What are we going to do Lana? I'm really scared for you."

"Not waste a single minute," she said, fingering the locket. "If we spend all of our time worrying about it we will both be miserable. I think the best thing we can do is spend as much time with each other as possible regardless of what's going to happen. That would make me happy."

"I have a great little place I want to take you when you come to my house. A picnic near the stream behind my house."

"Sounds romantic."

"It is."

There was a sudden knock on the door. We both froze.

"Lana is Patrick staying for dinner?" Her mother asked through the door.

"Do you want to?" She said, holding back a laugh.

There we were, half naked on the bed…a great first impression.

"Sure, I'll just call my parents," I said, trying not to laugh myself.

"Yeah Mom, that sounds great."

"Dinner will be ready in about an hour," her mother said, walking back down the hall.

After her mom had left, when we were done cracking up, we looked into each other's eyes.

"They are giving me a lot of breathing room. Under normal conditions you probably wouldn't have made it past the living room the whole summer."

"I guess so, she didn't even try the door."

"Well, we have a whole hour. What do you want to do?"

"That's a no brainer," I said, moving in closer to kiss her.

For the next half hour, we rolled around on the bed with each other. We gave each other massages. We kissed each other's bodies. When we were finished, we put our shirts back on and straightened out the bed.

"Let's open up the door," Lana said. "I don't want to take too much for granted."

"Good idea."

"Oh guess what. I have something for you."

She went over to the dresser and pulled a film envelope from the top drawer. I sat back down on the edge of the bed.

"You had them developed already?"

"My parents did, while I was in the hospital."

"Wonderful."

"I have my picture of you for the yearbook now," she said, sitting on the bed next to me.

She handed me the envelope. I took the pictures out and started looking through them.

"You took pictures of the meals they served you?"

"Those are evidence. I'm thinking of suing the hospital."

"On what grounds?"

"They were supposed to be helping me get better, not making me sick."

"Good point. You'll win hands down."

"Each food tray is like a still life. They each have a title. I'm going to put them all together in my album."

"There's the Seafood Newburg," I said, looking at a picture. "What's that one called?"

"Technicolor Yawn."

"Nice shot of the Beef Wellington."

"That one's called Bad Dog."

"What's this one? Oh, wait. That must be the Chicken au Gratin."

"Yeah right. It's called, The one that fell out of the nest."

I continued to flip through the pictures.

"Who's this handsome guy holding the tray?"

"The one posing as the Statue of Liberty? That's you."

"This is not going into the yearbook next year."

"Say's who?"

"Me."

"Oh, I'm shaking in my boots. I think it's a great idea to show everyone at school that you're paying your debt to society. It's a testimony showing that our judicial system is working."

"It's embarrassing."

"Deal with it buddy boy," she said, snatching the pictures out of my hand and putting them away. "Well, it's almost dinnertime. Let's go out and sit on the couch."

We went out to the living room and sat down on the couch hand in hand. Her father was in the recliner on the other side of the room reading the paper. I looked at Lana. Her hair was a mess. I could only imagine what mine must look like. I leaned over to Lana and whispered, so her father wouldn't hear me.

"You look like you combed your hair with a pillow. It's obvious that we just finished roughing each other up."

She looked at my hair.

"Yours looks like you've been driving with the top down…and your shirt is on inside out and backwards."

I looked down at my shirt. She was pulling my leg. We both started laughing wildly. She messed up my hair some more and took off running toward her bedroom. I chased after her. After some wrestling around with each other on her bed, we fixed ourselves up proper, and returned to the couch were we sat down and tried to keep straight faces. Her parents never said a word. Her mother continued to fix dinner in the kitchen while her father would glance over to us from time to time, smile, and go back to reading his paper.

I had a nice dinner with her family. I never mentioned Lana's condition and neither did anyone else. It seemed we all needed a normal moment from the last week's events. I politely answered her parent's questions about my family and everywhere we lived. Lana and me couldn't keep our eyes off each other. Sitting directly across from each other, we played with each other's feet under the table. I realized right there at the Meyer's dinner table that I was stone cold sober and loving life. I was crazy for the pretty girl who was sitting across from me. I wondered where her brother was, but kept the curiosity to myself. I think that for the briefest moment we all forgot how sick Lana was. When supper was over, I helped Lana clear the table.

"You're so damn polite," she whispered to me.

"I told you, I wasn't raised by wolves."

"And funny too."

"Patrick would you like some Ice Cream for dessert?" Her mother asked.

"I'll take a rain check on that on account that I'm stuffed from dinner. Thanks for the offer though Mrs. M."

"Mrs. M?" Lana mouthed, behind her mothers back.

We both had a good laugh over that one.

"What's so funny?" Her mother asked.

We both just looked at each other and shrugged our shoulders.

"Patrick let's go watch T.V. in my room."

"Sounds good to me."

We went back to Lana's room and left the door open this time. Lana turned on the television and we stretched out on her bed. She put her hands up to her temples.

"What's wrong?" I asked.

"Oh, these headaches. They seem to be coming on more frequently. The doctors said it might happen like this. I can get through most of the day without getting one, but then they start bothering me after dinner time."

"What about the medicine they were giving you at the hospital?"

"It's really strong. I get so tired after I take it. I'm only going to use it right before bed."

I thought of some questions that I wanted to ask Lana. I thought better of it. I wouldn't press her to talk about her condition. I took her hand and held it tightly in mine.

"If you ever need to talk to me about anything Lana, I'm here for you. I'm not going to mention it much. I would rather try to keep you happy and your mind off of things."

"I don't like talking about it much either. I had so much fun today I had forgotten all about things until the headache came along."

We lay there holding hands and watching television for a while. Her mother stopped at the door at one point and asked how Lana was feeling and if we wanted anything. For the most part, we were left alone to cuddle with each other.

"You must have been one heck of a baseball player."

"Why do you say that?" I asked.

"You made it all the way to second base today. Why didn't you try and steal third?"

"I thought I might get picked off."

"I doubt it. I feel so comfortable around you. It's as if we known each other for years."

"I thought you said you were shy?"

"I am…but it's different with you."

"Do you know how crazy I am about you?" I said.

"Only half as crazy as I am about you."

"It's going to be a great summer. I think it's about time I started for home, so you can get some rest."

"You're going to leave poor little old me all alone again?"

"Not because I want to. I'm not working at the restaurant until Wednesday. If you want, we can spend the whole day together at my house tomorrow. We'll be all alone until my parents get home from work."

"Sounds great."

"I'll talk to my parents when I get home and give you a call."

"Super. Let me walk you out."

I said my goodbyes to her parents, who were in the living room, and we walked out the door into a beautiful summer evening. We sat down on the front steps and talked for a little while longer. I finally kissed her goodnight and walked over to my bike.

"I'll call you when I get home."

"I can't wait."

"Bye Venus."

"Goodbye Mars."

I headed off down the driveway. When I arrived home, my parents asked me how things went. I couldn't have been happier. I mentioned that we planned to spend the day together tomorrow at our house.

"We could pick her up in the morning before I go to work and she could stay for dinner if you like," my mother offered.

"That sounds great Mom. I didn't want her riding her bike anyway; she needs to be taking it easy. I'll give her a call and let her know."

I called Lana and she agreed. We would have the whole day together alone. The next morning my mother woke me up at six thirty. I called Lana to make sure she was awake and getting ready. We picked her up at seven fifteen. I sat in the back seat, so Lana could sit up front with my mother. They talked up a storm all the way back to my house. My mother would look at me from time to time in the rear view mirror. I could tell she knew how special Lana was. They also discussed Lana's condition, my mother offering both advice and support. In no time we were home and my mother dropped us off at the top of the driveway, turned around, and headed off to work. She tooted the horn as she pulled off. Her and Lana waved goodbye to each other.

"She's very nice, Lana said, as the car went out of view. She must be an excellent nurse too, she knows everything about my treatments."

She turned and looked at the house. You could just make out the brook flowing behind it from the top of the driveway.

"Wow, it's beautiful."

"Not nearly as much as you are."

I took her backpack out of her hand and kissed her for a very long time right there in the middle of the driveway. When we were finished, she took the camera that was hanging around her neck and started taking pictures.

"So, what would you like to do first?"

"Can we go for a walk?"

"Sure. Let's put your stuff inside first and I'll take you to my little spot...it's across the brook."

We went inside. Lana met my father, who was getting ready to leave for work. I gave her the grand tour.

"This house was built from all of the pine trees that grew on the property," I explained to her, while showing her the living room.

"I love it here," she said, looking out the window into the water.

"There's a nice view from outside my room," I said, as I opened the door to the downstairs.

She followed me down the stairs. I put her knapsack down on the bed and went over to open the back door.

"This is so nice. You're so lucky."

We stepped out into the fresh summer morning. The air was thick with the scent of dew and clean running water. Lana looked down into the brook.

"It's so peaceful here. Is your spot over there?" She said, pointing across the water.

"Straight across and about fifty feet into the woods. There are no homes on that side. I think the land is a bird sanctuary and will never be developed."

"What's this place you want to take me to like?"

"There's a small clearing with pine needles on the ground. The pine trees form a perfect circle. You can hear the water moving along. It's a nice shady spot."

"Can we go over now? How will we get across?"

"There is a place a few hundred feet down where we can cross on several large boulders."

"Sounds like fun. Do we need to take anything with us?"

"Well, it's early…it's still a little chilly. We can take some blankets and pillows if you want. We can also bring something to eat and make a picnic out of it."

"It will be so romantic. Will we need this?"

She reached into her pocket and pulled out a single condom. I turned red.

"Oh, now look who's shy," she said.

"Shy and embarrassed are two different things."

"What have you got to be embarrassed about? I'm sure you know how to work Mr. Bojangles just fine."

"Mr. Bojangles? Who in their right mind names a penis Mr. Bojangles?"

"I do. I think it's a cute name."

"Penis's aren't cute, they're rugged. Field mice are cute. Tigers are rugged."

"Excuse me…Hmm…let me see. Tony or Mr. Bojangles?"

"Who the heck is Tony?"

"The only tiger I know is named Tony. It just doesn't sound right. Mr. Bojangles it is."

"Whatever"

She slipped around behind me and locked her arms around my waist.

"I'm so glad to be here with you," she whispered in my ear.

"You're like a dream come true to me. I still can't believe that we're together," I said.

"Patrick?"

"Yes babe?"

"I'm scared."

"Me too, but I'm right here by your side every step of the way."

"I get tired so easily…and the headaches will start up after dinner sometime."

"Just let me know if you need to take it easy or if you feel like going home. I'll take my brother's car if I have to."

She moved around in front of me and held both of my hands.

"I might need to rest for a little while later on, but I think I'll be alright."

"Anything you want angel face. We'll take a nap together."

I kissed her forehead and we stood there holding hands, looking into each other's eyes. Suddenly she perked up.

"Okay, I'm ready. Let's go."

"Let's get some blankets and pillows and something to eat," I suggested.

We went inside and she looked around my room while I gathered up two pillows and a couple of blankets. I put everything into a large beach bag and we went upstairs. She walked around looking at various things we had collected from living overseas.

"What kind of sandwiches do you want me to make?" I said, stepping into the kitchen.

"My favorite is tuna fish."

"Tuna fish it is then."

"This is an egg? It's huge. What's it from?" She asked, from the living room.

"An ostrich, we brought it back from Africa."

"I would have never guessed."

I finished the sandwiches, took two ginger ales out of the fridge, and put everything in my knapsack with some napkins. Lana continued to wander around the house in amazement. I could hear her taking pictures.

"Well, everything's ready. Do you need anything from your bag?"

"No, I'm just going to bring my trusty camera," she said, taking one more picture and then hurrying over to me. "I love it here."

"I'm glad, you're going to be spending a lot of time here with me this summer."

"Suits me fine. There are so many interesting things around your house and I love the location."

"Do you have to use the bathroom? We could be over there for a while."

"I'm potty trained don't worry."

"You're so fresh," I said, putting on my knapsack and picking up the beach bag.

We headed out and I locked the front door behind us.

"Now that's funny," she said, watching me.

"What?"

"One of the biggest thieves in town locks his own front door."

"Hey, you never know."

"Someone should rob you, so you know what it feels like."

"We were robbed once before when we lived in New Mexico."

"What did they take?"

"My mother's wedding dress. Go figure."

"I bet that marriage never lasted."

"Probably not."

We walked over to the trail that ran alongside the water.

"Where do we cross?"

"Right here!" I yelled, dropping the pillows and blankets.

I scooped her up in my arms and started to carry her toward the water. When we came to the edge, I started to swing her as if I was going to throw her in the water.

"Mars, if I so much as get one drop of water on me!"

"Hmm. To throw her in or not to throw her in? That is the question."

"I mean it…just one drop and you're dead."

"Let me see…death or dishonor?"

"I'm wearing my camera!"

"I'll buy you a new one. What's the magic word?"

"Please?"

"Please what?"

"Please Mr. Bojangles?" She said in the sweetest voice.

I started laughing so hard I had to put her down. She took a picture of me and patted the camera as if it was the top of a child's head.

"You would have ruined my baby," she said, looking at her camera.

"I thought I was your baby?"

"If I had to choose between you and my camera, the camera wins hands down."

"Well, at least I know where I stand," I said, picking up the beach bag and joining her on the trail. "There's a spot just ahead. See the large rocks in the water?"

"Yes"

"That's how we get to the other side. I'll take everything over first and come back to help you if you need it."

"My hero."

"My pleasure."

We crossed the water without anyone getting wet and made our way down to the point across from my house. Lana looked up to the house.

"They built your house on the perfect spot. It's very picturesque here," she said, taking a few pictures.

"Now we just need to go straight back about fifty feet or so."

"I'm ready when you are," she said, letting the camera hang from her neck again.

We started into the woods and walked for a brief period. Before long, we stepped into the middle of the circle of pines. Lana looked up and all around. She closed her eyes and inhaled deep through her nose. She exhaled, opened her eyes, and looked around some more.

"Perfect. Excellent choice. How did you say you found this place?"

"Just out for a walk one day after talking to you."

"Sure beats getting stoned."

"Yeah I guess so. Let's put the blankets down."

I put the pillows down and spread out the blankets while Lana watched from outside the circle.

"How do you suppose the trees ended up in a perfect circle like this?" She asked, as she picked up the pillows and placed them next to each other on the blanket.

"Just one of Mother Natures many miracles," I theorized.

"I guess so," she said, making herself comfortable.

"Are you cold?" I asked. "It's still pretty early."

"A little. Let's take off our sneakers, get under the top blanket, and take this all in."

We took off our sneakers and slipped underneath the blanket, resting our heads on the pillows. She pulled the blanket up around our necks. We lay there and looked to the sky and the tops of the trees. We held hands. We kissed. We discussed most everything except for her condition.

"Let's get undressed," she said, after a peaceful moment of listening to the water flow nearby. "But let's make a game out of it. You can't get up or out from under the blanket. Sunlight will burn us. We have to undress each other from underneath the blanket."

"Do I get to make any rules?"

"Sure go ahead."

"I get to take one item of clothing off of you, and then you have to take one off of me, and so on…and no talking."

"Okay good. Remember sunlight burns."

She pulled the blanket up over our heads.

"Where do you come up with this stuff?" I asked.

"I read my mom's Cosmopolitan magazines. I just put a little twist on it is all."

"What was the name of the article?"

"Oh I don't know…How to spice up a picnic between a thief and a drama queen. Do you want to play or not?"

"I never knew Cosmo was so hip," I said, reaching for her.

When I found her sides I began to tickle her wildly. She shrieked. She tried to get me back, but I blocked her with one hand and continued to tickle her with the other.

"Okay. Okay," she surrendered.

I decided to help her wiggle out of her shirt. She turned around and started with one of my socks, careful not to expose herself from under the blanket. I took off one of her socks; she pulled off my other one. I took off her last sock and she turned around again to help me out of my shirt. She turned her back to me and I undid her brassiere and I managed to wrangle her free from it. She was spinning around like a whirling dervish. I felt a tug at the bottom of my shorts. She was trying to pull them off. A hand came out of nowhere, unbuttoned my shorts, and unzipped me. I felt a couple more tugs, this time harder. I lifted myself a little while she pulled like crazy. We were laughing pretty good, but neither one of us said a word. When the shorts finally came off, she shot out of the end of the blanket like a cannonball.

Her head and shoulders were exposed to the light and she howled in mock terror. Diving back under, she pulled the blanket half off me in the process. We ended up laughing and screaming wildly. No matter how hard we both tried to get back under, the blanket seemed to small. If sunlight burned, we both were fried to a crisp. I finally pulled her shorts off and it was all downhill from there. She pulled off my boxer shorts and I slid off her panties. When we were finished, we both came up for fresh air and looked at each other laughing.

"That was perhaps the most interesting thing I've ever done," I said, out of breath.

"Patrick, do you want to make love to me?" She asked me, as casually as if she wanted to know what my favorite color was.

"Of course sweetheart."

"I don't know, I'm feeling a little less than attractive these last few days."

"You're as pretty as the first day we met. Nothing's changed."

"Are you sure?"

"Positive."

I was learning to think how others might feel. I moved closer, so we could kiss. With that, we were into each other's arms. Flesh consuming flesh. We played with our tongues. We touched each other's faces. Her mouth tasted like some edible flower dripping with nectar. We played like this for a while, hands reaching and touching across each other's bodies. She retrieved the condom from her shorts and handed it to me. I placed it on myself. She instructed me to move to the center of the blanket. She put her full weight on me and we kissed each other like that for a while. Before I knew it, she was guiding me toward her with her hand. I could feel myself being swallowed by the heat of her body. We were insane with desire for each other. I thought I might go mad.

If there was any pain, she never said a word. I was as gentle as I could be, falling slowly into her rhythm. It was everything I dreamed it would be and more. We spoke to each other through our bodies, riding the wave of emotions that consumed us. She was wearing nothing except my locket and we were making love. Every once in a while she would let out a little moan that twisted itself around the sound of the running water and was carried off into the treetops.

I didn't think I could hold out for one minute longer when her body suddenly went rigid. We exploded inside of each other. We buried ourselves into each other's necks. We shivered. We shook off our passion inside of each other. When we finished, she collapsed on top of me. We traded kisses. We gazed into each other's eyes. We were soul mates, forever joined by this one act. We traded pieces of our souls with each other. We breathed in each other's breath. We were one.

"That was so perfect," she said.

She lifted herself off me and snuggled up next to me.

"Turn on your side, so I can lie against your back," she whispered in my ear.

We rested there like that in the summer morning, both spent and breathing heavy. Our bodies were pressed against each other. Her arm was draped around me. We stayed like that until our breathing was replaced with the sounds of the birds and the gurgle of the brook. Over the melody of the world coming to life around us, I could just make out the sound of Lana softly crying. I squeezed her hand.

"I'm right here baby. I'm not going anywhere."

I did not ask her why she was crying because deep down inside, I knew. I had to be strong. I gently caressed her hand to let her know I knew how she was feeling. She was scared. We both were. After a few minutes, she finally spoke to me.

"Got a cigarette?"

"You're kidding, right?" I said, spinning around to face her.

"That's what they do in the movies."

"How about a sandwich instead?"

"If that's all you have, I guess it will have to do."

"You're something else, you know that?" I said.

"You're not so bad yourself Mister," she said, winking at me.

That was how we lost ourselves to each other that summer morning. We dressed, and had our picnic in the shade of the middle of the circle of pines. When we arrived back at my house, it was almost noon.

"Would you like to take a hot shower?" I asked, setting everything down on the living room floor.

"With or without you?"

"I'll join you as soon as I put everything in the wash. Let me get you something to wear in the meantime."

"Sounds great," she said, setting her camera on the windowsill by the couch. "It's amazing. You can't see our little spot from here...but it's so close."

"Not with all the leaves on the trees. It's just far enough back. Our own little secret."

We went into the bathroom. I turned on the shower for her and showed her where everything was. I waited until she stepped inside and I picked up her clothes. I went downstairs, changed clothes, and filled the washer machine. I picked out some sweats and one of my concert tee shirts for Lana. I went back upstairs and joined her in the shower. We soaped each other up and took turns rinsing. I watched her as she rinsed off. I kissed her back as she washed away the remains of our lovemaking. I never felt so completely connected to anyone in my whole life.

"I put a towel and some clothes for you on the hamper. I'll finish up and be right out."

"Thank you sweetheart."

She stepped out of the shower. I rinsed off and joined her in the steam filled bathroom. She was fixing her hair in the mirror.

"Do you feel like taking a nap?"

"That would be wonderful," she said.

I dressed myself and we went downstairs. She went over to the bed and stretched out. I put the towels in the washer with our clothes and turned the machine on. I went back into the bedroom and cuddled next to her.

"Mars?"

"Yes Venus?"

"That was absolutely the most beautiful time we spent together this morning."

"I would have to agree with you on that."

"Except for one thing."

"What's that?" I asked.

"We were supposed to wait until we were married."

"Well, it's too late for that now...but I can arrange the marriage part if you would like."

"Really? How?"

"Just leave everything to me."

I left her on the bed to ponder that one. I went into the next room to check on the wash. I knew we could never get married now, we were way too young, but the thought was very appealing to me. I had other plans, a loophole if you will, that would secretly allow us to be married. Well, more or less. I went upstairs and brought a cold ginger ale down with me incase Lana was thirsty. When I returned to the bedroom Lana was fast asleep. I sat in the chair next to the bed and watched over her. My eyes filled with tears. It was my turn to cry.

That is how it would have to be. We would take turns. We were far too young for any of this. I slipped onto the bed and settled down as close as I could next to her. I rested my arm across her body. She stirred and reached for my hand. She smelled like strawberry and rainwater. My Venus. We both fell asleep with our hands clasped.

When I woke up, I went to put our clothes in the dryer. I stretched out next to Lana again and thought about everything that happened only hours earlier. I was truly blessed to be with this girl. When the dryer was finished, I woke Lana up and she changed back into her clothes. We tidied up the bed, folded the blankets, and put them away. We decided to go for a walk before my parents came home. Lana grabbed her camera and we headed out the door.

"So, how do you feel?" I asked, as we headed up to the dirt road in front of my house.

"Like a million dollars. I really needed that nap. Not only that, but you were so patient and gentle with me this morning. The perfect spot, the nicest guy…everything was just how I imagined it would be. I get chills just thinking about it."

"Why me Lana? I mean, you could have been with any guy you wanted in school. Why did you decide to go out with me?"

"Let's face it. You have a mug on you only a mother could love. If not me, then who?" She teased.

"C'mon Lana get serious for a minute."

"I am serious. Have you looked at your puss in the mirror lately?"

"Will you knock it off?" I pleaded.

"Knock what off? I'm afraid to look at you for too long. You might turn me into stone or something."

"That's it!"

I went for her waist and started to tickle her. She screamed and danced away from me.

"Okay, I'll cool it. You're such a big baby."

"I was thinking while I was watching you sleep. I feel so fortunate to be with you."

"You want to know the truth?" She asked.

"Of course"

"For starters, everyone in school knows you're a bad apple, but nobody said you weren't good looking. I guess I had a secret crush on you since I first saw you in school."

"Really?"

"You were so mysterious. Besides your looks, something else appealed to me. You were like the forbidden fruit. My friends would say, look, but don't touch. He's no good."

"What did you think when I first walked into your hospital room?"

"Besides, Oh my God, I think I'm going to have a heart attack? Well, I knew you were high as a kite."

"How could you tell?"

"Patrick, Visine may get the red out, but it doesn't do a damn thing for keeping your eyes open."

"That bad huh?"

"A set of toothpicks wouldn't have helped you. Even so, when you walked into the room, my heart skipped a beat."

"I can't believe it."

"Don't let it go to your head. All we need is you walking around with an inflated ego. Seriously though, after everything that's happened in the last week or so, you're still right here by my side. That's what really attracts me to you. It's not something you can see or touch. It's inside of you."

"What else would I be doing?"

"You could be doing all of those things you used to do before we met. Give yourself a little credit. You're changing everything about yourself, so we can be together. You can't imagine how that makes me feel."

"Hey Venus?" I said, as I pulled her close and put my arm around her.

"Yes Mars?"

"I love you."

"I love you more."

"Are you hungry?" I asked her.

"I could chew the arm off of a rag doll."

"Good. My mother should be home by the time we get back. I'm sure she will be cooking something wonderful for dinner."

"Yummy. I have a question for you Mars."

"Shoot."

"How in the world are you going to get us married? Surely, you were joking. It's not something you can send away for on the back of one of your comic books you know."

"I told you I would take care of it. Patience my lady."

"See what I mean…so mysterious."

We walked all the way down to the dam where the waterfall was. Lana took some pictures and we headed back to my house. When we walked in the front door, my mother was in the kitchen getting dinner ready. We sat in the living room and watched television. Lana and my mother chatted back and forth making small talk. My father came home from work shortly after that. My parents seemed to warm up to Lana quickly. It wasn't hard to do. I had an angel sitting in my living room and she was with me. Lana offered to help my mother with dinner and they were chatting away preparing dinner. My father settled down in his recliner with the evening paper. We discussed sports and how well the garden was doing this year. It was the most family time I had in years. It felt good.

My mother showed Lana how she made her lasagna and served it with fresh vegetables and a salad. It was Lana's turn to do most of the talking. She answered the usual questions about her family and background. Lana and my mother discussed her condition. My father and me talked about how to keep the animals from getting inside the garden and eating it up. By the time the meal was almost over, I knew that my parents were completely impressed with Lana. I couldn't help wondering if they were thinking, "What in the world are you doing with our son?" She was clearly out of my league. When we were all done eating, Lana began to help my mother clear the table.

"Lana you don't have to do that. Sit down. Relax," my mother said.

"It's okay. If I do nothing at all I get so tired."

My mother let her help.

"Patrick, what time do you want me to drive Lana home tonight?" My father asked, returning to his recliner.

Lana intercepted the question.

"Well, I have my first appointment at the hospital tomorrow in the morning to set up my chemotherapy. Your son, Jesse James, plum tuckered me out this morning," she said, winking at me. "How about in a half an hour?"

"That works for me," my father replied.

"Hey Mom, maybe you could ride along, so Dad and you can meet Lana's parent's real quick?"

"I don't see why not."

"You don't mind do you Dad?"

"Not at all."

We all piled into my mother's car and headed off to Lana's. Her parents were in the living room watching television. Our parents exchanged greetings and Lana's father offered to make drinks. While our folks were getting acquainted, Lana and me had some ice cream at the dining room table.

"They're getting along rather well," Lana said.

"What did you expect them to do, wrestle each other?"

"See, you're cute and funny...or is it funny looking and cute? Either way, that's why I like you so much."

We kissed each other and began to spoon-feed each other our ice cream. Neither one of us seemed concerned with what our parents might think. Lana started in with one of our role-plays in between spoonfuls of vanilla.

"Oh Dr. Killpatient?"

"Yes Miss Meyers?"

"You promised me a thorough examination as soon as I returned home. Have you forgotten?"

"Now is not the time or place. I am a professional. I have ethics and standards to uphold."

"I say now *is* the time *and* the place or you won't be up holding anything for the rest of our relationship except Mr. Bojangles."

"Idle threats will get you nowhere. See those people in the living room? Those are real people. They are our parents. I would lose my license to practice medicine for sure."

"No time like the present I always say. Where's your sense of adventure?"

She took a spoonful of my chocolate and missed my mouth on purpose, smearing it all over my face, then took off running for her bedroom. Our parents stopped talking and were now looking at me. I wiped my mouth with a napkin, smiled at them, and took off running after Lana. I could hear them laughing as I jumped on the bed next to her.

"Hi Doc."

"Hello Miss Meyers. I could lose my position at the hospital over this."

"Oh fiddlesticks."

"Alright you win. What can I do for you?"

"It hurts right here." She said, pointing to her lips.

I kissed her passionately.

"And here." She said, touching her neck.

I snuggled her and kissed her so much I gave her a slight hickey on her neck.

"And here."

She lifted her shirt up a little and touched her belly button. I couldn't resist. I stood up and leaned over her stomach and kissed her ever so gently on her navel, then gave her a raspberry. I blew way to hard and with the bedroom door open, the noise could have been heard in Kansas. We were both laughing so hard she almost fell off the bed. I quickly settled back down next to her and stifled my laugh with the pillow.

"Excuse me," I said, when I came up for air.

"Oh Dr. Killpatient…you're rotten. Haven't you any manners?" She said, waving the air around in front of her nose. "What did you eat today? My eyes are burning."

"Hospital food. Does it every time."

"I seriously hope you wash your own under shorts. Those are throwaways if not."

"Must have been the stuffed peppers…I'm sorry Miss Meyers."

"What did they stuff them with? Beatle dung? Oh my God! We can finish the exam later…right now you better go clean yourself up…and make an appointment to see the proctologist first thing in the morning."

"We'll do."

We were howling with laughter again.

"Is everything alright in there?" Lana's father shouted from the living room.

When we finally calmed down, we made ourselves comfortable on the bed again.

"This is great. Now we can see each other all of the time without our parents worrying. It's going to be a great summer," she said.

"Count on it. Now perhaps my parents will let me drive my brother's car. I hate riding my bike everywhere."

"Your brother lets you drive his car?"

"Only while he's away in the military. I'm supposed to be saving for my own."

"I get to drive my mother's car whenever I want," she said.

"Good. If my parents let me drive my brother's car, we should have no problem getting around. Fourth of July is right around the corner. I figure we could go to the fireworks at the beach."

"Oh, that would be so nice. I want to go up to the Old Man of the Mountain too. There are a lot of trails up there. Have you been?"

"No, not yet. We'll add it to our list."

We made plans for our summer together while our parents were drinking whisky sours in the other room. After our parents met, the sky was the limit. We could spend as much time at each other's house as we wanted. I was told that night on the ride home that I could use my brother's car when I needed it. Lana was welcome to come over to our house anytime. Things were looking up.

Independence Day fell on a Saturday, I had permission to skip my community service at the hospital and take Lana to Hampton

Beach for the fireworks. Lana spent most of the day sleeping, hoping that she would feel well enough to stay up late into the evening. I spent the day over at her house checking up on her from time to time. While she slept, I washed and waxed my brother's car. I also spent a lot of time sitting in the chair in her room looking through the photo albums that she had made since receiving her first camera at the age of twelve.

She was an excellent photographer. It really amazed me how talented she was. She put her heart and soul into everything she did, including our relationship. Lana woke up at four in the afternoon. I had the car packed and was ready to leave. I waited as she showered and dressed for the beach. When she returned to her room, she packed up her camera and a few other things she wanted to bring.

"How do you feel sweetheart?" I asked.

"So far, so good. I can't wait to get to the beach and watch the sunset with you from our blanket."

"Weather's perfect for it. Not a cloud in the sky."

"What else do I need?" She said, stuffing items into her beach bag.

"I think you forgot the kitchen sink. We are only going to the beach for the evening."

"Watch your tone Mister. A girl needs to have whatever she wants when she's away from home for a week, day, hour or minute."

"I'll go rent a truck then."

"Keep it up and you'll be eating burnt hot dogs and washing them down with unsweetened lemonade in my back yard instead of going to the beach. You'll be waving a sparkler around trying to fight off the mosquitoes"

"Okay. Okay. Get whatever you need."

"Thank you. Let's see…I need this…and this."

She jammed a few more items into the bag. She checked my face to make sure it remained expressionless.

"Who's going to carry all of this stuff anyway? I've got a ton of crap in the car already."

"Why you are, of course."

"Wonderful."

"Don't tell me the honeymoon's over already?" She teased.

"We're not even married yet!"

"You promised you would take care of it."

"I'm working on it. Are you almost ready? Perhaps it would be easier to bring the beach to us?"

"I'll ignore that last comment. Would you be a dear and carry my bag to the car while I finish up here?" She said, dropping the bag on the bed and walking out of the room with her nose in the air.

"Yes Miss Meyers. I'll get right to it."

We were on the road a little after five o'clock. It was almost an hour drive to the beach. We drove with the windows down and the music turned up. We sang all of the songs that we knew together. When we arrived at the beach, we decided to cruise the strip and see if there was any metered parking right on the water. We would settle for one of the lots a block or two away from the water if we couldn't find a spot after a few passes.

"I hope for your sake we find an open meter…there's an awful lot of things to carry!" She said, slapping the dashboard and laughing to herself.

"The first thing I'm going to do when I park this car is carry you down to the ocean and throw you in."

"If one drop of water touches me buddy boy, you'll pay."

"Yeah. Yeah. I've heard the threats before. This time, I'm willing to pay the consequences."

She stuck her lower lip out and pouted. She was wearing a pair of cotton Capri pants and one of my many concert tee shirts she had on permanent loan from me. She was also wearing an oversized beach hat and a pair of sunglasses. To complete the look, she had picked out a nice pair of sandals. Even dressed down for the beach, she was a total knockout.

"That car's leaving up there!" She screamed, pointing and waving wildly.

"I see it, I'm not blind you know."

I put my blinker on and waited. The parking meter Gods were smiling down on us today. I pulled in, put the full eight hours on the meter, and opened the door for her. She stepped out into the salty sunshine and looked around.

"Hey, there's an arcade right across the street. I hope they have Pac Man. I love that game."

"I'm sure they do." I said, looking into the back seat and wondering what I was going to carry first.

"Let's put our blanket out first and put our stuff on it. Then we can walk around for a while," she suggested.

"Our stuff?"

She put her hands on her hips, cocked her head to one side, and glared at me.

"Excuse me Miss Meyers. I meant to say, right this way to your blanket."

"That's better," she said, grabbing the big bag she packed for herself out of the back. "Can you handle the rest?"

"No problem Miss. Step right this way and wait by the railing."

I gathered up the blanket, cooler, towels, and beach bag. I locked the car up and turned around to face her. She had a big smile on her face.

"Something funny Miss Meyers?"

"I was just thinking, you sure do bring a ton of stuff for one day at the beach."

"These are the necessities. We could have a yard sale on the beach with everything you packed into that bag of yours."

I marched by her and over to the set of stairs leading down to the sand. I stopped at the bottom and turned to see if Lana still had that smirk on her face. She was pearly whites from ear to ear.

"There's no red carpet Miss Meyers. Would you like me to secure a spot and come back and carry you?"

I almost broke character with a big smile myself. If I were going to play the act, well then, she would let me. She called me on my offer.

"That will do just fine. Make sure you get a good spot, not too close to the other blankets…and not too far from these stairs. I'll be waiting here."

"Yes M'am! I'll be right back."

I started into the sand and found a nice spot not too close to anyone else and in direct line from the stairs. I spread everything out and looked over to Lana.

"Oh Jerome!" She yelled to me. "You forgot my bag," she hollered, holding it out to the summer air.

I stomped back over to her on the bottom stair and took the bag from her.

"Who's Jerome?"

"Why you are…combination butler, bodyguard, and my part time lover."

"Why Jerome?"

"Oh, I don't know. I like the name is all," she said, looking away with an air of dignity.

"Part time lover?"

"Full time lovers require a much better level of service."

"Yes M'am!"

I took her bag over to our spot and dumped it out in the middle of the blanket. I messed everything up with my hands. I folded all four corners of the blanket to the center, picked it up, and gave it a couple good shakes. I set it back down and patted the top of the pile with my hands. I returned to Lana, scooped her up, and started to make my way across the sand.

"How's that for service?"

"Why I never," she said, smiling at me. "I've had better service at a filthy gas station."

"Sorry Miss, doing the best I can."

We both started laughing like two crazy people. I almost dropped her on the way back to the blanket, we were laughing so hard. When I set her down, she looked out to the ocean and back toward the car. It was a perfect location. We fixed up the blanket for the evening and repacked her bag. We sat down next to each other and took off our shirts. She was wearing a nice red bathing suit top underneath her shirt. I couldn't take my eyes off her.

"This is a perfect location. Would you get the sun block out of my bag and put some on my back. I'll burn up to a crisp if I don't use it."

"Can I put some on your front too?"

"You're so fresh."

"Just asking. What do you want to do first?" I said, fishing through her bag for the sun block.

"Let's go down to the water and look for some shells. I want to find something unusual, so I can remember this day."

"Sounds like a plan. Let's get this sunscreen on you, so you don't turn into a lobster while we are doing it."

I covered her back with lotion and rubbed it in. While she was covering the rest of her body, I took off my sneakers and put them on the lower corners of the blanket. When Lana was finished, she took off her sandals and placed them on the top two corners. I put some tanning lotion on myself and we were ready to go.

"Do you want me to get your back?" She asked.

"Sure," I said, turning my back to her.

"There," she said, rubbing in the last of the lotion. "You're all set. Find a marker, so we can locate the blanket on the way back."

We stood up and looked back toward the car.

"There's the arcade and we're right across from it, straight out from the stairs. Do you want me to lock your camera up in the car?"

"No way," she said, putting it around her neck. "How am I going to take pictures if the camera is in the car?"

"Just checking. Let's go then."

I gave her a quick kiss and took her hand in mine. We went straight down to the water and started looking for shells.

"Keep your eyes open for sea glass too. I want a shell and a piece of sea glass."

We walked hand in hand on the edge of the surf and looked around. There was nothing except broken shells in the sand. We strolled along the edge of the water until we came to a small jetty of rocks. The pieces of shell seemed to be more abundant here. There were pools of water in between the large rocks that had been left behind by the last high tide. We were looking around the large boulders when I spotted an unbroken shell.

"Hey, look at this!"

I reached down and pulled it up out of the wet sand. It was a spiral shell with a bright red line of color wrapped around it.

"That's the one," she said, taking it out of my hand to examine it. "Now if we could find a nice worn piece of glass to complete our collection."

"Leave it to me," I said, looking around the tide pools again.

We started walking back toward our blanket. I was looking down for the most part, but every so often, I would look up ahead of us. When I looked up the next time, I couldn't believe what I saw.

"Oh no."

"What?" Lana said, intently looking down for her piece of glass.

"Here come your best friends."

They were about a hundred feet from us, heading directly toward us. As far as I could tell, they were looking right at us. One of them pointed in our direction.

"Looks like the cat is finally out of the bag. Where's my Nixon mask when I really need it?" Lana said.

"Do you want me to let go of your hand?"

"Hell no. Hold me close and kiss me."

That is exactly what I did as her friends approached us. I didn't see their faces while I was kissing Lana, but she told me later it was priceless. The three of them looked like they had just witnessed the second coming of Christ. Her best friend Michelle was the first one to say something when they stopped in front of us.

"Lana Meyers and Patrick Fisher? What are you two doing here together? Well, I can see what you're doing. I mean...Lana, I wouldn't believe it if I wasn't seeing it with my own two eyes."

Her other two friends, Tammy and Angela, stood there like bookends on each side of Michelle, lifting up their sunglasses to have a look at us. For the first time since I had met Lana, she was speechless. There was a long moment of silence while Michelle's interrogation hung in the air like smog. The crashing of the waves on the beach marked what seemed to be an eternity of awkwardness. It was time for a public service announcement.

"Ladies and Gentlemen," I said, looking at Lana's friends and anyone that was within earshot.

"I would like to bring your attention to the main attraction. In the center ring here we have Lana Meyers and Patrick Fisher."

Some of the people nearby had stopped to listen.

"They are officially going steady… you heard me right…boyfriend and girlfriend. That's right folks…they're best friends…they're lovers. They spend late nights on the phone whispering sweet nothings into each other's ears. Don't crowd the stage ladies."

I shooed Lana's friends back with a few sweeps of my hand like a circus ringleader.

"Let everyone get a good look. No flash photography please."

I put my arms around Lana and gave her a kiss like we were just married. A few people who had stopped to listen were clapping. Lana's friend's jaws were almost touching the sand. When I was done kissing Lana, I turned toward her friends and took a bow. Lana took my cue and took a few bows herself. The bookend on the right, Tammy, was the first to speak.

"Lana why didn't you tell us?"

"I didn't think anyone would understand."

"How on earth did you two meet?" Angela asked, while Michelle was still picking her jaw up out of the sand.

"We met in the hospital. He's really so sweet," she said, looking at me while I nodded my head up and down in approval.

"Now I know why I can never get you on the phone anymore, and I thought it was because you were sick," Michelle finally said.

"What are you all doing now?" Lana asked.

"We came for the fireworks," Tammy said.

"So did we. Our blanket is just a little ways up. Would you ladies like to join us?" I asked, trying to fit in.

"Sure," Michelle said. "I've got to get the scoop on this story. This is front-page news. Lana Meyers and Patrick Fisher. Holy crap."

She gave Lana a look.

"You little devil."

I looked down at my feet for a brief moment and there it was...a piece of glass. I bent down to pick it up and held it out for everyone to see.

"There's the sea glass you wanted my dear."

"Oh Patrick it's beautiful," she said, taking it from my hand. "This looks like it was a piece of a Coke bottle. See the color?"

Everyone looked at it. She put it away in her pocket with the shell and kissed me on the cheek.

"This is definitely going to take some getting used to," Angela said.

"It will be painless. I promise," I said to her. "Anybody hungry? I'm buying," I said to everyone.

"We're starved," Michelle said.

"Me too," Lana added.

"Good, let's move your blankets next to ours, head up to the boardwalk, and get something to eat. Sound like a plan?" I said to Lana's friends.

"Sure," they all answered in unison, and then looked at each other and laughed.

We gathered up the their blankets and I helped them carry everything over to our spot on the beach. As it turns out, they were less than a hundred feet from us. We set everything up for the night and went up to Ocean Boulevard where all of the arcades and food vendors were. We decided on a place that had something everyone wanted. I let the girls order first, then placed my order, and paid for all of it. Everyone thanked me as I handed out the meals. We decided to eat on the blankets and watch all the boats that were dropping anchor a little way out in the ocean.

During the meal, Lana and me told the story of how we met and fell in love with each other. The girls asked questions and one of us would answer them. We told jokes and laughed. We walked along the beach. We talked amongst each other until the sky turned shades of violet and crimson. Before I knew it, I was getting along quite well with Lana's circle of friends.

We had a while before the fireworks started, so we decided to go up to the arcade and play video games. I personally spent some time with each one of Lana's friends getting to know them a little better. Every time Lana looked at me, she winked. I really don't think I could take all of the credit for how well me and Lana's friends hit it off. These girls loved Lana. They knew she was sick. If I was making her happy, all things considered, then it must have been alright by them.

We all sat down on the blankets and waited for the fireworks to begin. As I sat there looking toward the sky, I had the feeling as if I finally fit in somewhere that mattered. I had a whole new set of friends...all girls. Lucky me. As we all looked toward the sky, a quiet moment came over us as a single small rocket went up. I turned and gave Lana a long kiss and reached for her hand. When we were finished we both said, "I love you." Her friends all laughed, then the night sky was painted with bright vivid colors.

The fireworks were spectacular. We all commented as each group went off. Lana took pictures. As the grand finale exploded into the night sky, I moved as close to Lana as I could. I couldn't help a few teardrops escape from my eyes and roll down the side of my face. I didn't want any of this to end. God please help my little angel.

Afterwards, traffic leaving was rather heavy, so we sat and talked on the blankets. We joked and laughed until Lana felt the first sign of a headache coming on. She kissed all her friends goodbye. I walked her up to the car, opened her door, put the keys in the ignition, and turned the radio on. I picked her up and set her on the hood of the car.

"Get some fresh air. I'm going to get our things. I'll be right back."

"Mars?" She said, throwing her arms around my neck.

"Yes Venus?"

"I'm so happy to be with you. You were a perfect gentleman tonight. My friends are actually jealous as hell."

"You think so?"

"I know so. They all told me."

"I couldn't have done it without you. I will be right back. Here, let me help you into the car. I'll put the window down a little for you. You rest while I go get our things."

"Thank you Mars."

I shut the car door for her. I walked back to the blanket to pick up our stuff and say goodbye to my new friends. The girls were still chatting away when I returned.

"Patrick, you're so good to her," Michelle said. "I guess we had you figured out all wrong."

"No, you had me figured out correctly, but that girl is changing me. Every minute I spend with her I see a whole new way of life," I said, as I gathered everything up in my arms. "It was a pleasure meeting all of you."

"I hope we can hang out with you guys again," Michelle said.

"Do you all like to go hiking?"

"We love it," Tammy said.

"Lana and me are driving up to the Old Man of the Mountain this coming Thursday. Would you like to join us?"

"Sure."

"Great."

"Sounds like fun."

"I'll make sure she calls all of you before then. We can all fit into my brother's car. Well, I have to get my baby home to bed before her headache gets much worse."

"Take good care of her for us Patrick," Angela said.

"I wouldn't think of anything less. Goodnight and drive home safely tonight."

I walked away with my head held high. When I returned to the car, Lana was fast asleep. I set everything down on the sidewalk, opened her door, and put the seatbelt on her. I unlocked the back door, loaded everything into the back seat, made my way around to the driver's side of the car, and quietly climbed in behind the wheel. I drove us home and listened to the radio. Every once in a while, I turned to look at Lana sitting next to me. I loved her so much that it hurt.

Before I knew it, Thursday was here. I was so busy between Lana, work, and the hospital that the days seemed to be flying by. It was six in the morning and I had to pick up Lana and her friends in an hour. I showered, dressed, and called Lana to make sure she was feeling well enough to go. The hiking trip was a success. We all had a great time and took a ton of pictures. If there were any doubts about me, this may have been the turning point. By the end of the day, it seemed like we had all been friends for years. This only helped Lana's and my situation, for we were finally able to relax, and not worry so much about being seen together.

Everyday that we spent together was an opportunity to get to know each other better. As it turns out, we had a lot more in common than we originally thought. We owned the same rock albums. We both loved sports and the outdoors. It was hard to tell who was the bigger neat freak. One of us was always role playing or hamming it up. Many of the things that we shared I had long since forgotten about and replaced them with doing drugs. Now that I wasn't using anymore it was like experiencing things for the first time all over again.

We settled into a routine of seeing each other almost every day. During the week, we spent time at either one of our houses. We were usually alone. Our parents accommodated us without any questions or concerns. Lana had her transfusions moved to Saturday mornings, so we could spend time with each other before my shift at the hospital. I would drive her to the hospital and her parents would take her home and put her to bed when she was finished. On Sunday, she would rest at home and talk to her friends on the phone to let them know how she was doing. Sunday was a good day for me to catch up on things around the house and spend time with my parents. I would do yard work or gardening with my father or help my mother around the house.

Lana's parents always followed us in their car to the hospital on Saturday mornings. During this last infusion, Lana's parents wanted me to join them for the doctor's consultation while Lana was getting her procedure. It wasn't good news. The cancer was still spreading at a swift rate and there were now new growths detected on the last brain scan. They had moved her condition up to a stage four. With her dosage of chemotherapy already at the maximum toxicity, there was little to do except wait and hope for a change in her condition.

The doctors explained that recovery to a certain extent was a state of mind. If we decided to tell Lana that things were getting worse, she might give up her positive attitude. Everything is relevant, the doctors explained. A positive mental outlook couldn't do anything to hurt her chances of fighting the cancer. I wanted to ask the doctors a million questions that were swirling around in my head, but I could not utter a word. I must have been in shock. I suppose I just wanted to know if I was going to lose my girl to this terrible disease. This was all really too much for me to handle, and I excused myself, so I could get some air. Afterwards, we all agreed not to tell Lana of the new findings. We needed to be strong, so she could continue to be strong.

After that weekend, we started to do all sorts of things with her friends. We all went for walks, to the movies, roller-skating, and to yard sales and flea markets. We all loved the flea markets. We would see who could find the most unusual item priced less than five dollars. Some mornings I would pick everyone up before dawn and we would drive out to the beach just to watch the sunrise and have breakfast. If I was working or doing my shifts at the hospital, I made sure that at least one of her friends spent time with her. I wanted her to always be surrounded by her friends and me, so she would keep her mind off things as much as possible.

I knew Lana's parents were in constant contact with the specialists, but I never asked her parents what her current condition was. If I was to remain strong for her, I didn't want to know any more bad news. I figured that if things started to turn around, Lana's parents would let me know. The time we all spent with Lana was so much fun it was easy to forget about what was really going on.

As July turned into August, Lana's condition was worsening. Her headaches were coming on stronger and earlier in the day. Her afternoon naps were getting longer. Her hair began to fall out whenever she brushed it. She began to take her pain medication in the late afternoon because she couldn't wait until bedtime. Lana's best hours were early in the mornings. She would have several peaceful hours before she needed to rest. I continued to take her to the hospital for her infusions. I couldn't bear to listen to the doctors tell Lana's parents what I already knew. She was not getting any better. It was obvious.

Sometimes I would spend the night in the rocking chair by Lana's bed reading and watching her sleep. Part of me didn't want to face the truth about her condition. Lana was the strong one. She knew how she felt, and that it wasn't getting any better. Nobody needed to tell her. I was feeling so many emotions that it often felt like I was on a roller coaster. The highs were the good times spent with Lana and her friends. The lows were when I let everything get into my head, and was overcome with sadness and worry.

I prayed at night for Lana. I prayed for that miracle. I promised I would stay on the right track if somehow she could be saved. Some nights after we hung up the phone, I would cry myself to sleep. I talked to my parents. I talked to our friends. I even talked with my probation officer. Lana's parents often tried to comfort me on those nights I spent over their house watching Lana sleep. Nothing seemed to brighten the darkness that had settled over my heart. I couldn't talk to Lana about it. She had no trouble discussing it with me.

It was an early summer morning in August and we just arrived at my house after spending the night at Lana's home. Lana wanted to be alone with me at the circle of pines. My father was just coming out of the house to go to work.

"Don't lock it Dad," I said, coming down the driveway with Lana.

"Good morning," he said, looking up at us. "How are you this morning Lana?"

"Early mornings are the best time for me these days Mr. Fisher."

"Well, I'll see you kids later," he said, walking up to his truck.

Lana waved goodbye as he backed out of the driveway. My father didn't seem the slightest bit concerned that I was just getting in from Lana's house. As long as I called and let my parents know what was going on, I could do whatever I wanted with Lana. In fact, he rather enjoyed it when Lana and her friends were over the house. He would cook hamburgers and hot dogs on the grill for us, and make a nice steak for himself and my mother. He was used to all of us downstairs making noise or outside raising hell. These days it was early in the morning when we all gathered at my house. We would sit around the kitchen table and decide what to do while my parents got ready and left for work. It felt good to be trusted again. They knew I was in good hands anyway.

"Well, we're all alone," I said, as I closed the door behind us.

"Good because I have a surprise for you."

"That's funny because I have one for you as well," I said.

We went downstairs to my room and I opened the back door.

"Patrick can we go to the circle today? I feel well enough."

"Sure, as long as you feel up to it."

"There is something we have to do first. I want you to help me cut my hair today. It's starting to come out in clumps when I brush it. I will feel better when it's gone. I already have patches missing here and there anyway.

"Whatever you want sweetheart."

"Do you have a hat I can wear until I get used to it?"

"Sure, I've got several baseball hats in my closet."

"From what teams?" She said, sitting on the edge of the bed.

I went over to the closet and pulled out my hats. I brought them over to her.

"There's Boston, Baltimore, and a Yankees hat."

"Yankees!" She said, making the sign of the cross with her fingers. "Back...get back you traitor."

"What? You know I lived in New York for years. My aunt still has the house there."

"Take me home Benedict Arnold," she said, crossing her arms and looking away.

"Without your surprise? Okay, what ever you want."

"Oh never mind, I'll get over it. Give me the Red Sox hat."

"I thought you'd see it my way."

"I thought you'd see it my way," she mimicked.

I dropped the hats on the carpet and tackled her on the bed. One thing led to another, and we made love for the first time in my room. It was nothing short of spectacular. After we caught our breath and dressed, we were ready to cut her hair.

"Do you have an extension cord?" She asked.

"Check."

"We're going to need a mirror too."

"Double check."

I gathered up the items from around my room along with a towel to put around her shoulders. We went outside and I ran over to the shed to fetch a lawn chair for her. I brought it back and set it up, so she was facing the water. I placed the towel around her shoulders and went back inside to get the extension cord and the mirror.

"Are you sure you want to do this right now?" I said to her through the screen door.

"Yes Patrick."

I knew by now, that when she used my first name, she meant business. I plugged in the cord, ran it out the back door, and handed her the mirror. She handed me the clippers from her bag and set the bag down next to her. I plugged in the clippers and turned them on to make sure they were working properly.

"What setting do you want me to put these on?"

"Three I guess. I am going to wear the hat most of the time anyways. At least I won't be completely bald."

"Whenever you're ready," I said.

"I'm as ready as I'll ever be."

"Okay. Here I go."

I turned on the clippers and ran the blade across her head from front to back. Her hair fell to the ground in several small piles. I made seven or eight more passes with the blades and had most of the hair off her head. I noticed several small spots where the hair had completely fallen out.

"Lean forward a little please."

"Will you kindly stop with the polite Sweeny Todd barber act and get on with it?" She said.

"You know, one good push and you'd be right down there in the brook," I teased.

"You're always threatening to throw me in the water somewhere. I've already been baptized. Now let's get on with it...chop chop."

"Now let's get on with it...chop chop," I said under my breath, making a face to the back of her head.

"Excuse me?" She said, watching my every move in the mirror.

"Sorry Miss, just one more minute. I need to touch it up is all," I said to her reflection in the mirror.

"That's more like it. It's so hard to find good help these days," she said, leaning forward.

I finished the back of her head and then propped her head back up with my fingers. I made a few more passes to make sure I didn't miss anything. I turned off the clippers and unplugged them. She looked at herself in the mirror.

"I guess I won't be going anywhere without the hat," She said, scrunching her nose up.

"You're still gorgeous."

"Yeah right."

"Why don't you take a quick shower to get the hair off of you?"

"Good idea. Then we can go to the circle. Will you join me?"

"As soon as I'm done cleaning this up."

"Don't be too long, I need you to wash my back."

"How come I never get to wash your front?"

"You have to earn that privilege."

"I'm trying…believe me."

She went inside while I cleaned everything up. When I was done, I gathered up the usual blankets and pillows and then joined her in the shower. It suddenly occurred to me that we always showered together. The well wouldn't be running dry any time soon. She finished up before me and made her way back downstairs. When I joined her, she was wearing the baseball cap.

"Are we ready to go?" She asked.

"I just need to grab a couple of ginger ales and some snacks," I said, getting dressed.

"Hey, where's my surprise?"

"Where's mine?" I shot back.

"We cut my hair. Surprise!" She said, taking off the cap to show me. "What did you get me?" She asked.

"Ponytail holders."

"Real funny wise guy. C'mon you can tell me."

"I'm going to give it to you when we get over to the pines."

"Well then, let's get out of here. I can't wait."

We went upstairs and packed up something to eat and drink. It was another beautiful day. The stream was at its lowest level of the year and we had no trouble crossing. When we arrived at the circle, we spread out the blankets, and put the pillows down. We stretched out and looked up into the treetops.

"You know, this is my favorite thing to do. It's so peaceful here," she said, getting comfortable.

"You're so beautiful," I whispered into her ear.

"Do you still think so?" She said, fingering her locket.

"Always…I have something for you."

I reached into my pocket, produced a small velvet box, and handed it to her. She bolted upright.

"For me? Oh Mars, you shouldn't have."

Lana loved surprises. As I watched her, it was hard not to be caught up in her positive energy. She was radiant. She opened the box and looked inside. There were two gold bands staring her in the face.

"Oh my God. They are beautiful."

"They're from a company called Black Hills Gold. It's fourteen karat yellow, rose, and white gold."

"I love the leaf designs on them," she said, taking the smaller one out and slipping it on her left ring finger. "It fits perfect," she said, holding it up to the light. "How did you know my size?"

"I took one of your rings out of your jewelry box while you were sleeping. Your mom told me where to look."

She took my ring out and set the box down. I held out my left hand and she slid the ring on.

"I now pronounce us husband and wife. I told you I would take care of things."

Her eyes welled up with tears, so I sat up and kissed her. We held each other tightly for a long while.

"You're so good to me Patrick. Thank you."

"Take your ring off for a minute."

"No way. I'm never going to take this off."

"I want to show you something."

She reluctantly slid the ring off her finger.

"Look inside of it." I said.

On the inside of the ring, there was an engraving. In block letters, it said: VENUS AND MARS – FOREVER. Mine had the same inscription.

"Oh my God. I love it. That's so nice," she said, quickly putting the ring back on her finger. "Mars, you sure do know how to charm the pants off a girl don't you?"

"I promised you I would get us married. So, now were married."

"My mother knows you were going to buy wedding bands?"

"She knows I was going to buy you a ring is all. I needed your size though, so that's how she became involved. You can tell her we're married when you get home."

"You and my mother are thick as thieves. She really likes you Patrick."

"What's not to like?"

"You're so full of yourself," she said, holding her hand out and admiring the band again. "Oh Jerome?" She said in her blue blood voice.

"Yes Miss Meyers?"

"Would you like to consummate this marriage?"

"Plum tuckered out right now. Have one of your other part time lovers fill in for me, will you?"

She slapped the side of my leg and pushed me. We fooled around for a while in the soft warmth of the circle of pines. When we were finished, she sat up, and opened the ginger ales.

"Patrick, do you think you will stay off the drugs after I'm gone?"

Oh boy. Here we go.

"You're not going anywhere," I said, trying to sound convincing.

"We both know my condition is worsening. My parents leveled with me. I know about the new growths."

"We decided not to tell you when it was discovered, so you would keep a positive attitude. I should have told you, but I thought it might help if you didn't know."

"I don't blame you. I would have done the same thing."

She set the can of soda down and pulled her legs close to her chest.

"What are you planning to do after high school? Have you thought about college or the military like your father?"

I swallowed hard.

"I'm not sure."

I really didn't have a clue. I suddenly realized that most of the kids my age were thinking about grades and planning for college or something else.

"You have a full year of school left. You could get the grades to get you into almost any school you wanted. Your mother tells me you could get straight A's without even cracking the books when you apply yourself."

I just sat there and listened to her. Something told me she wasn't quite finished just yet.

"Promise me that you will go on and do the things that I will not have the chance to," she said, turning to face me and clutching her knees again.

"C'mon Lana. Don't say that."

My throat was closing over. I looked at my ring. Who knew how much time we had left together? I was waiting for a miracle. I was waiting for the doctors to tell me something different. She was facing the truth. I was running from it. Her dreams of going to Berkeley and studying music were not going to materialize.

"You can't just go back to what you were doing after I'm gone and expect your life to fall into place. You will end up in prison, or worse."

"I'll figure it out Lana. I won't let you down."

"At some point you're going to have to want to do all of this for yourself. You have made a lot of progress so far. The hardest part of your journey will come after I'm gone."

"I'm fine Lana."

"You're fine now. After I am gone, you are going to be going through a lot emotionally. I don't know how I would handle it if I lost you. You have to promise me that you won't quit. You have to give this new life for yourself a chance to grow and blossom."

"I will sweetheart," I said, looking away. I was struggling not to break down.

"Life is precious…look at what we've shared together in just this short time. It wouldn't be fair to yourself to waste it after I'm gone. If you're not strong enough to do it for yourself, do it for me until you are."

She took her hand and moved my chin back toward her, so that we were looking at each other again.

"Someday you're going to go on and meet someone and have a family. Let's face it, that someone is not going to be me."

"Lana stop…please," I whispered.

"Please let me continue Patrick."

"I'm sorry."

"The way I look at it is this…God has other plans for me. I have accepted that. My days are numbered. You have your whole life ahead of you."

She started to play with her ring. I took a sip of ginger ale and tried to steady my nerves.

"If you waste your life, then we have two tragedies. Take the feeling you have for us and run with it. Let it inspire you to do great things. Don't look back. Find a dream for yourself and hold on tight."

I thought that at any minute I was going to lose it. She was saying her goodbyes. My Venus was going to leave me soon. Please Lord, stop this from happening to us. I needed air.

"This summer has been the best thing that ever happened to me Patrick. It's exactly how I dreamed my first love would be. You have changed so much. Don't stop changing after I'm gone."

I started to say something and she put her finger to my lips. She took my hand and held it. Tears were now rolling down my cheeks.

"It's okay. Cry. Let it out."

As hard as I fought to remain in control of my emotions, the tears kept coming. Wordless drops of salty water falling to the blanket below me.

"Do you know what I think?" She finally said.

"What's that?" I sniffed.

"God owes me a favor…a big one. When the time is right I will send you a sign to let you know that it's alright…to let you know I'm doing well and that it's time to move on."

I thought about that.

"What would the sign be?" I wondered aloud.

"Let's just say that when you see it, there will be no mistake that it's from me."

She smiled. I pondered the possibilities. I was raised to believe in a loving God. The request of hers was certainly within almighty power. I listened to the soft music of the flowing brook. I looked at my angel.

"I promise," I finally said. "I'll do my very best."

I meant it with all my heart. I would stay on the right track. I would make something of myself. I would grow up. After a nap and an early dinner with my family, I drove Lana home. On the way back to my house, I thought about everything she had said. It was my wakeup call. If she left me and I returned to my old ways, what would become of me? I couldn't go back to the life I was living and expect to make it in the real world. That much was now obvious to me. I had been in a fog for so long that I never thought of the future. I had to have Lana shake the truth into me. My parents had tried to do the same thing with me, but Lana was different. I could talk to her. I was just learning how to communicate with my parents again. I had a lot to learn. The truth was that Lana's departure would be my arrival if I wanted it bad enough. I was learning to see through new eyes. I had hope for the future.

As August waned on, Lana's condition grew worse. On the mornings where she had slept the night before, she would insist that we go to the circle of pines and talk. Her friends would often visit early in the mornings when she felt well enough. Some days she was too sick to get out of her bed. Her pain medication would have put me down for the count. I would sit in the rocking chair by her bed and keep watch over her. I would read to her. I would tell her stories. I would wipe her mouth if she was sick and I would cry when she slept.

Her parents and relatives were always in and out of her room. No one ever asked me to leave or step out of the room. I sat there next to her day in and day out. Sometimes I would hold her hand and sit on the bed with her. I could tell she was losing a lot of weight. The ring that I had bought for her was loose now. When I wasn't working, I spent most nights sleeping in the rocking chair. I kept my family informed of her condition. Sometimes, my parents would show up at her house to check up on her. Our parents would sit in the living room and discuss Lana's situation. I think we all knew that the end was near.

The subject was never brought up to me, but it was clear that she would not be returning to school with me. Lana was not going out without a fight though. She woke up one morning before Labor Day weekend and insisted that I take her to the circle one last time. Nobody could deny her request. Off to the circle of pines we went. I carried her out to my brother's car. When we arrived at my house she walked into my home on her own. My parents were getting ready to leave for work. She gave both of them a big hug. Somehow, I think she knew it was going to be the last time she would see them.

I gathered up the pillows, blankets, and some ginger ale. We walked down to the edge of the brook. Lana had amazing strength that day. She made it across to the other side without any help from me. When we arrived at the circle, I set everything up like we always did, and we stretched out.

"This is the last time I am going to see this place," she said, lying next to me on the pillows. "I wonder if there is a place like this where I'm going?"

"I'm sure there is sweetheart."

I couldn't do anything except hold her hand and try to keep my composure.

"Patrick, I wanted to come out here with you one last time, so I could thank you."

"You don't have to thank me for anything baby doll."

"Yes I do. For spending every possible minute that you could have with me."

"Lana I'm in love with you. Right now and always. Being with you is the best thing that has ever happened to me."

"There is something you don't know though," she quietly said. "When we first met at the hospital and started seeing each other it may have seemed like I was the one who had everything going on and I was giving you the chance to be with me."

"It's the truth. Who else would have given me the time of day?"

"Patrick, I was so afraid of relationships. I always used the excuse that I was too busy. It was so much more than that. Before I met you, I was very lonely and depressed."

"I never would have guessed. So, how did I end up being the lucky one?"

"I knew as soon as you walked into my room to collect my tray. I can't really explain it, I just knew. After we met on that first day, all of the fear and anxiety inside of me vanished."

"It must have been my cologne."

"Very funny. I just knew that there was a different side to you. I wasn't afraid anymore. I wanted to find out everything I could about you."

"Are you afraid now? You know, of everything that's going on now?"

"It's not dying that frightens me. It's being without you that I'm worried about."

"I'll always be right here," I said, touching her on her chest over her heart.

"I know," she said, as she took off her ring at looked at the letters inside. "Venus and Mars Forever," she said aloud. "You know, I was so flattered when I found out that you called me Venus around your friends."

"I couldn't believe it when you thought of Mars for my nickname."

"I should've called you Pluto. You were really a little further out in space back then. You were such a mess…so was I in other ways. I think we saved each other."

She put her ring back on her thin finger.

"Thank you Mars."

"You're most welcome Venus."

I leaned over and kissed her on the lips. Afterward she turned on her side to rest. I lay down next to her and pressed my body up against hers just the way she liked me to. She reached for my hand and draped it across her waist. I held her close to me as we drifted wayward on the morning sunshine. We slept together for a couple of hours. I drove her home at noon that day and she was never to return to my house.

At this point, her headaches were coming on in the early hours of the day and lasting throughout the night. She was taking so much medication that I often wondered how she kept her eyes open. I stayed with her all that night in the rocker by her bed. The next morning I drove home to take a shower and get a hold of myself. I needed to keep busy. I also wanted to give her parents some alone time with her.

I was a complete wreck at my house. I did my laundry and cleaned my room to try to keep my mind busy. While I was cleaning my room, I remembered the little fold of foil that had the drugs in it. I looked inside the record album and there it was at the bottom with the rest of my money. I took it out and placed it on the dresser. I had a promise to keep. Drugs had other plans for me. I called Lana's house. It was late in the afternoon. Her mother answered.

"Hello Mrs. Meyers…how's Lana?"

There was a long pause.

"Patrick?"

"Yes, I'm here."

I thought I was going to hear those words that I never wanted to hear. Not now. Not ever.

"The doctor just left. She will be lucky if she pulls through the weekend. She's unresponsive. Her breathing is weak. It's almost as if she's in a coma. We don't know if she's going to pull out of it."

"I need to come sit with her."

"Sure Patrick, whenever you're ready."

I waited for my parents to get home and had dinner with them. I cried in front of them. We said a prayer for Lana at the supper table. We held hands. We hadn't said a prayer at the dinner table since I don't know when. We were becoming a family again. My sister would be coming home Sunday afternoon. I actually missed her.

I was downstairs getting ready when it happened. I was hurting way too much inside and having trouble keeping my composure. I was exhausted. I was scared. I didn't want to lose my Venus. Drugs were the last thing I needed. It would only increase my emotions. I saw the piece of foil on my dresser where I left it. I carefully opened it and looked inside. Nine tiny pills. I dumped them out on the mirror that we used when we cut Lana's hair. I took one of them, carried the mirror out the back door, and flipped the rest of them down into the water. I caught my reflection in the mirror. It was grotesque. I hated what I saw and threw the mirror against the foundation of the house and it smashed into a hundred jagged pieces. I went back inside, grabbed the car keys, and drove directly to Lana's house.

When I arrived at Lana's house, I went directly to her room and took my place in the chair. Her mother and father were sitting on the bed with her.

"She hasn't opened her eyes since you left early this morning," her mother said.

"Perhaps she will hear you," Mr. Meyers said.

Her parents left the room. I could hear her mother break down as they walked down the hall. I sat on the bed next to her. I held her hand. I talked to her. I prayed that she would open her eyes. After a while, I went outside to sit on the front stairs. I couldn't bear to look at her like this. That is when it hit me. I had broken my promise. I felt guilty. After everything that Lana was going through, I couldn't keep my end of the bargain. I remembered what Lana had said about doing it for me. I realized, right then and there, that I had enough. A strange feeling came over me as I promised myself I would never get high again.

When I returned to Lana's room, her parents were just leaving. I sat on the bed next to her. I patted her forehead with a damp cloth. I needed something to keep my mind off things. Music. We used to argue about who the best rock band of all time was. She loved the Beatles. I favored Pink Floyd. Each of our choices seemed to reflect our personalities. She was a gentle breeze. I was a little rough around the edges. I opted for the second side of Dark Side of the Moon. As the music filled her room, I sat back down on the edge of the bed and watched over her. I was sitting next to her praying for a miracle when she gently stirred. Her eyes softly opened.

"Hi Mars."

"Hi Venus."

"Can you get me some water? Where are my pills? My head is killing me."

I found her pills on the bedside table and poured her a glass of water. I handed her a couple of pills and she took them. I gave her the cup and she drank from it. I watched her for a moment.

"Mars?" She whispered.

"Yes Venus?"

"You should have put on the Beatles," and she smiled at me.

"You've been out cold since after I left this morning. The doctor was here. I was so afraid I wouldn't speak to you again."

"You know I wouldn't leave you without saying goodbye. I was having the strangest dream. I was calling you, but you couldn't hear me. You were lost in the woods. I was at the circle of pines and there was snow on the ground."

"It's okay, I'm here now."

"That's the funny thing…when I was calling out to you I started getting scared. Then I looked at my ring and touched it with my other hand. That's when I opened my eyes and saw you sitting on my bed."

"I'm never going to leave you Lana. You will always be right here."

I touched myself on the chest above my heart.

"Can I sit on your lap for a little while in the rocking chair?"

"Sure sweetheart."

I stood up on the side of the bed, leaned over, and lifted her out of it. She was so light. She looked up at me and smiled again. I went over to the rocker and sat down with her in my arms. We just rocked back and forth and looked at each other.

"Patrick, hand me the picture frame with the flowers you gave me in it."

"Okay. Put your arms around my neck for a moment."

She held onto me while I reached for the picture frame. She took the frame from my hand and I put my arm around her again.

"These are my favorite gifts that you ever gave to me."

"I know."

"I took a petal off of each flower and put them in my locket, so I will always have them with me…see?"

I looked at the two flowers in the picture frame. Each one was missing a single petal.

"Do you think we are soul mates?" She asked.

"Venus and Mars forever," I said.

"You're going to do the right thing. I just know it. You have to do it for yourself now."

"I know. I will."

I was going to lose it. My whole body was shaking. I tried to hold my breath, but I was shivering with her in my arms. She reached up and touched my cheek. She brushed a tear away.

"Promise me?"

"I do."

She closed her eyes for the last time. I just didn't know it then. I was trying to keep my composure. I kissed her head and gently rocked the chair. I closed my own eyes to try to stop the flow of tears. At some point, I had rocked myself to sleep and she stopped breathing. She dropped the picture frame to the floor and I started to dream strange colorful things. Her parents found us in the rocker just a short while later.

When her father picked her up off my lap, they discovered that she had passed away. I had been born. I had a second chance at life. Her father put her down on the bed and both her parents collapsed in tears. I kissed her one last time on the lips, touched her locket and ring, and whispered to her, "I'm right here." I touched her on the chest above her heart and I knelt down on the side of the bed with her parents and cried like a newborn baby.

I never went to Lana's funeral. I couldn't hold it together long enough to walk out the front door. I also did not want to tarnish her memory by being with her family at the service. Only a few people knew of the changes that I had made over the summer. I told her parents I was too sick with grief. They said they understood. Her brother even called to thank me for taking such good care of his sister. Her parents told me when I was ready to visit Lana's grave, to please contact them first. I promised to do so, and told them I would be in touch.

Everyone seemed to understand what I was going through except for me. Everybody said the same things to try to comfort me. My thoughts on the subject were different. First loves are unique. They change and shape a person. They are magical. All passion and moonbeams. A first love is full of feelings, emotions, and thoughts. We are experiencing something new, something that we have dreamed about for so long that is finally coming to fruition. These relationships are held together with desire, clasped hands, and late night phone calls. When Lana left me, I didn't think I would ever get over the pain. I just didn't think it was possible.

She will be a part of everything that I do right down to my final day when I will close my eyes for the last time and meet my maker. A piece of my soul is missing forever. I believe that our creator wired us to be with one mate for life, like swans. I would eventually move on, but the past will always be somewhere just under the surface.

I did not keep the promise I made to Lana about the drugs, but I did keep the one I made to myself on her front steps the night she passed away. I never forgave myself for that…for getting high on the day she passed away. It took me a while to realize that I had to be true to myself before I could be honest with someone else. I was learning so many lessons.

My old friends didn't seem to want to have anything to do with me when school started. To be honest the feeling was mutual. When we did run into each other in school, it was, at best, awkward. Word had gotten around the school about Lana and me, but nobody ever mentioned it to my face. I pretty much kept to myself. I would talk to Lana's girlfriends in class and in passing, but I still felt alienated from the kids that had their heads on straight. I heard that my old friends were picked up for new robbery charges and possession of firearms at the end of summer. They were all awaiting court dates and would be tried as adults this time. I was so grateful to have not played a role in of any of it.

I ended up graduating with excellent grades for my last year of high school. Instead of scrambling to get into a college, I decided to enroll at Bard College in upstate New York. My grandmother and aunt live in a house that is surrounded by the college campus. The house was built in 1851, and the family history goes back in the area even further than that. My aunt has worked for the college her entire life and is in charge of Central Services at the school. There would be no tuition, and I could live in the house where I spent so many summers growing up under my grandmother's watchful eye.

Before I left for New York, I spent some time over the early summer hanging out with Lana's girlfriends. We would all meet and go to the beach or hiking. We always ended up talking about Lana and remembering the good times we had together. This would re-open the wounds I was trying so desperately to heal. After several weeks, I decided to leave for New York. Perhaps I thought I could run from the pain and memories that haunted me.

I had one thing left to do before I left, and that was to visit Lana's parents. I decided it was time to tell them the whole story about my past and how I was changing. I called them on the phone and set up the meeting for the weekend. It was a hot Sunday afternoon when I arrived at their house. Just seeing her house tore me apart on the insides. We sat at the dining room table drinking iced tea. After the small talk and before I could get to what I wanted to tell them, Lana's mother said she had something she needed to read to me. It was a letter to them, written by Lana, before she lost her battle to cancer.

The letter told the story about how we met. It described everything Lana knew about my past, and the incredible changes I had made over the summer. She wrote about how I took such good care of her, making her last days special and worthwhile. By the end of the letter, I knew I was heading for another breakdown. I steadied myself and tightened every muscle in my body, fighting for control over my emotions. Lana was gone, and yet, here she was being the strong one. Lana's parents had known about my past for quite some time now. They must have believed in me too.

"Have you been to the gravesite yet?" Her father asked.

"No, not yet. I'm still working up the courage."

"Well, when you decide to go, please let us know in advance."

That was the second time they asked me to do that. The truth was, I wasn't sure if I would ever have the strength to go to the cemetery. I finished my iced tea and there were hugs and kisses.

"I'll let you know how college goes."

"You'll do fine. I'm sure of it," her mother said, as I left the house.

I had one close call with alcohol and drugs before I left for my grandmother's house that summer. I was desperately lonely. I missed Lana. The waves of grief ripped through my body like a tornado. I took a pint of whiskey from the bar at home. I drove to Manchester, picked up a few joints from the pool hall, and headed off to Hampton Beach in my brother's car. It was late at night when I arrived at the beach. I slept in the back seat and when I woke up it was almost sunrise. I grabbed my blanket and shoved the whiskey in the front pocket of my shorts.

I went to the exact spot where Lana and me watched many sunsets, sunrises, and the fireworks. I watched the sun come up from my blanket and then walked along the beach in the cool morning light. I ended up throwing the marijuana into the ocean. The whiskey I saved to remind me of how close I am to losing everything again. It stays in a box downstairs in the closet at my father's house.

On my first day of college, I was running very late for my afternoon class. When I arrived at the lecture hall, I could see a full house through the window. The teacher was standing next to an overhead projector; he looked like he was ready to begin. I opened the door and couldn't see any open seats, so I was forced to head down the stairs in front of everyone. I could feel all eyes on me. I nervously looked around for an empty seat. I dropped a book. I thought I heard someone laugh.

"There's an empty seat over here."

I couldn't make eye contact with anyone. I picked up my book, turned in the direction of the voice, and saw the open chair. I hurried over and sat down.

"Are you okay?" I heard the girl next to me whisper.

When I turned to my right, I saw her. She was beautiful. She was wearing a pink angora sweater. She was twirling her hair with her index finger. The sign.

"I am now."

I smiled at her and she smiled back. I never said another word to her until class was over. Every time I glanced over at her, she was looking at me. After class, we ate dinner together in the cafeteria, and had coffee in the snack shop. We talked for hours getting to know each other. She was enrolled as a music major with an interest in photography. When we were finished, I walked her past my house to her dorm. I told her of my family history in the area. When we arrived at her room, I told her it would be nice if we could get to know each other better. She said she felt the same way. Before I left for home I gave her a quick kiss on the cheek goodbye. She had no objections.

*   *   *

It has now been almost thirty years since Lana passed away. I have been happily married for over twenty of them. Her name is Lynn.

She is the girl I met on the first day of college. We have two children. Lynn knows everything about my past. She knows about Lana and our summer of love. She thinks it is nothing short of amazing. Sometimes when I am lost thinking about the past, she knows where I have drifted off to in my mind. She tells me I need closure. I have yet to visit Lana's grave. I have not returned to my mother's either. She lived long enough to see her grandchildren. Cancer also took her away from me.

I have used every excuse not to go to the cemetery for many years. I think the truth lies in the fact that I was dishonest with her on the day she passed away. The guilt of getting high while she was on her deathbed has been eating me up from the inside ever since. It was as if I tarnished all the time we had spent together with one selfish act. A normal person will find it hard to hurt someone without experiencing a similar amount of guilt. It is one of the many balances within our universe.

I hurt everyone around me with my behavior and drugs...family, friends, victims, and even Lana. After the initial thrill was over, I would have to say that I used drugs to be able to live with my conscience. Sorry just doesn't cut it when you keep doing the same things over and over again. Words needed to be followed by an appropriate amount of action over time. I needed to let her know I never did forget her. I also needed to get honest with her about the night she passed away.

Near the end, she always said I would meet someone and have a family. I owe Lana praise for everything I have and cherish today. The odds of me turning my life around before I met her were slim to none. She was the one who planted the seed of hope in my heart and watched it grow while her own inner light was fading. She was patient, kind, and understanding. It was her commitment to me in my darkest hour of need that allowed me to rise up from the ashes of the miserable life that I was living. I was to learn selflessness, so I could be with her in her time of need.

*   *   *

Somewhere underneath the bad in most drug addicts is a good person trying to break free. Lana was an expert in seeing the bright side of people and bringing those qualities to the surface. She took a chance on me, when anyone else with half her sensibility, would have turned and run the other way. The decision for me to change was only made possible by the guiding and unconditional love of someone stronger than I was. I realize today that those helping hands were always around me, reaching out to save me from myself. Drugs clouded my ability to see, hear, feel, taste, and touch. Love was the only thing in all of creation that had the chance to return me to sanity.

For the first time in many years, the old demons have come calling me again. I have been having thoughts about getting high. Things in my life couldn't be brighter at this moment in time. From my discussions with others about the subject, I am told that is how it can happen. From the depths of hell, out of nowhere, you can be blindsided and right back where you started. I have been talking to my wife about what has been going on in my head, and she mentions that it might be time to visit Lana's grave.

I called my father and asked him to take me to the cemetery. It is late November. We decided that December 7 was a good day, the anniversary of my mother's death. The day before, I drive to New Hampshire to my father's house. A bedroom is still downstairs, everything the way it was left almost thirty years ago. My father uses it as a guest bedroom when he has company. In the wardrobe, there is a few of my father's summer clothes hanging in there, and the box I left on the shelf many years ago.

After a nice meal with my father, I do the dishes and go downstairs for the night. I have a big day tomorrow. I take the box out and bring it over to the bed. I take the top off the box. The pint of whiskey is staring me in the face. I take it out and set it on the bed. There are countless pictures that Lana and our friends have taken. I spend until early in the morning looking at each one and reliving the memories. It tears my heart out to look at some of them. I cry for the first time in a long time.

When I am done looking at the pictures, the box is empty except for a lock of Lana's hair that I saved from the day we cut it off. There is also a small velvet box. I pick up the hair and twirl it around my finger. Lana was always twirling her hair with her finger. I smell the ringlet of hair and I swear it smells like rainwater and strawberries. The small velvet box is the only item left in the carton. I can't bear to open it up and see the ring, so I pack everything up, and put it back in the closet. My thoughts as I drift off to sleep are that I am finally going to make peace with Lana, or perhaps, with myself.

It snowed several inches while we were sleeping, and I woke up to see everything covered in white. I made my way upstairs to find my father getting dressed. I made us some breakfast and did the dishes afterward. I remembered that I needed to call Lana's parents and let them know I was going to the cemetery. I spoke to Lana's mother and she asked me to stop in along the way. I made it a point to call them at least once a year when my family was visiting my father. Lana's parents have even met my wife and children. The last thing I need to do before we leave is call Lynn. I tell her I am leaving for the cemetery with my father. She tells me I am finally going to find the missing piece of the puzzle that makes up my life.

We started out on the back roads of New Hampshire in my father's truck. I remember a time when these roads were unpaved and there were fewer houses. The view with everything freshly covered in snow is still the same…it is breathtaking. We pulled into the driveway and I tell my father I will be right out. Lana's parents were waiting for me and quickly answered the door. I slip my boots off at the mat and take a seat on the sofa.

"Lana wanted us to give you this before the funeral. It was one of her requests," Mrs. Meyers quietly spoke.

She handed me a small picture frame. I took it from her hand and looked at it. The two flowers I had given Lana when we met at the hospital were inside of it. The color had faded from them somewhat, but they were full of vivid memories.

"She wanted you to bring these to her one last time. There's a small weatherproof box on the right side of her headstone, you can place it in there."

"Thank you," I said.

"Her stone is around back in section E. If you're standing with your back to the road, it's on the left side near the small tree," Mr. Meyers said.

"One more thing," her mother spoke up. "Thank you for taking care of our daughter. She loved you so much."

"The pleasure was all mine. I have a great life thanks to Lana. She believed in me when almost nobody else did. I still don't know how I won her over."

"That girl was always so full of surprises," her father added.

"Well, my father is waiting in the truck. It's the anniversary of my mothers death today, so he is coming along as well."

I stood up. I gave Lana's mom a kiss, shook her fathers hand, and looked him in the eyes.

"Happy Holidays. I'll be in touch."

"We love hearing from you," her father said, while I put my boots on and opened the door.

"Goodbye," I said, stepping out the door and into the snow.

We backed out of the driveway and headed toward route 128. The cemetery was on the left just a little past my old high school. My father glanced at the picture frame in my hand. He never said a word. I gazed out the windshield somewhere beyond the road ahead. I was having second thoughts. There would be no turning back now. I looked over to my father. Nerves of steel, I thought. We pulled into the cemetery and drove around back. I could see the tree off to the left when my father stopped the truck.

"See that one right there?" He said, pointing out my window. "That's your mother's. Do you remember?"

This was not going to be easy.

"Are you ready?" He asked, opening his door.

"Sure Dad," I lied, and opened mine.

When I stepped down onto the ground it was as if I just awoke from a long dream. The sunlight was bright. My eyes hurt. The snow twinkled like a billion diamonds. I kept blinking like a kitten testing new eyes. I watched my father as he pushed the snow off my mother's stone. He stood there with his head down. I made my way over behind my father.

"Hi mama. I finally came to see you and Lana."

I didn't know what else to say, so I wandered from my father, so he could have a moment alone and I could find Lana. The picture frame was hanging from my hand as I headed toward the tree. As I approached, I could see an older marker and the name read Myers. I looked to the next marker, which stood several feet away, and closer to the tree. It was a large heart, shaped out of rose-colored granite. I worked my way over, carefully stepping between the stones along the way. I stood directly in front of the large stone heart.

I could see the name Lana and the last few letters of Meyers; the snow was covering the rest. I stepped forward and brushed the snow away. The gravestone read: Lana "Venus" Meyers. There was a picture etched into the stone of the likeness of the Greek Goddess. The dates were also inscribed. My hands started to tremble. I broke down. I found the weatherproof box on the right of the stone and brushed the snow away. I opened the lid, placed the flowers inside, and snapped the lid closed again.

"These are for you. Sorry it took me so long to bring them."

I didn't know if I was talking in my head or whispering to her on the gentle breeze. It did not matter. The flowers were always Lana's favorite gift from me. I gave Lana all types of gifts that summer; none of them was more special than these two flowers. "It's the little things," she would say. As I stood in front of her, I realized that I had grown into everything she wanted me to be. I was doing the best that any mortal man could do. Others were depending on me now. I had a purpose in life. Tears were streaming down my face. I couldn't breath. I could hear my father come up behind me. I looked over to my mother's grave. They were so close.

"You two watch over each other," I said.

"Are you alright son?" My father asked.

I took a deep breath. I was a wreck.

"Yeah Dad, I'm fine."

I lied again. Some things never change. I turned to my father with tears in my eyes.

"Dad?"

"Yes son?"

He looked at me for a long time and patiently waited for me to answer him. When I could speak again, I said, "Do you ever miss Mom so much that you just break down and cry?"

"All the time," he replied.

I thought about my father crying over my mother, his first love. I realized then that I could have always talked to my parents, I never tried, and then blamed them for it.

"How did you manage to go on after Mom died?"

"One foot in front of the other I reckon. Some days it has to be that simple. One foot in front of the other."

My parents were married for forty-five years when my mother passed away. I only knew Lana for a few months. I figured, all things considered, we were about even. We were both missing a piece of our souls. I thought about Little League baseball and my dad never missing a game. I was beginning to understand what was important in life.

"Dad, what do you say we do a little fishing this spring and catch a Red Sox game?"

"I would like that very much Patrick"

I looked back to Lana. I didn't need to explain anything to her about the night she passed away. Something inside me told me she already knew. She also knew how sorry I was that it ever happened. I was so sorry that everything I did wrong happened. I needed to forgive myself. Everyone else had forgiven me long ago. I had my answers. I walked over to my dad. He put his arm around my shoulder and we started for the truck. I was growing up. I would always be growing up.

Sometimes growing up hurts. Through that hurt, I would heal, and grow some more. "I miss you Mom. I miss you Venus. You two watch over each other."

When I returned home with my father I said I had something to do before we went out for a bite to eat. I went downstairs. I pulled the box off the closet shelf. I opened it. Out of a small velvet box, I pulled out a ring. I looked at it. Lana's girlfriends said she was buried wearing her locket and ring. I put it in my pocket. I looked at the whisky bottle. I shook my head. I don't need you anymore. I put the top on the box and put it away. I went out the back door and around to the shed. I found something to dig with. I made my way along the brook and carefully crossed on the snow-covered rocks. I worked my way back upstream to the circle of pines. I had not been there since the last time with Lana, the day before she passed away.

I stepped into the middle of the circle and cleared the snow away with my boot. I dug a hole a few inches down and placed the ring in it. I put the dirt back and covered it with frozen pine needles then snow. I stood up and looked toward my father's house. With no leaves on the trees, I could just make it out through the branches. I lingered for a moment. I thought of warm summer mornings and being with Lana on a carpet of pine needles. I felt warm. I stepped out of the circle and into the cold wind and started to make my way back home.

I had just crossed over to the other side when I suddenly stopped. I didn't feel right. Something was terribly wrong. I turned and went back to the circle of pines as fast as I could. I dropped to my knees and started digging frantically with my bare hands. I found the ring. I looked at it in the winter light of day. I read the inscription. Venus and Mars Forever. I put the ring on my finger next to my wedding band. At that moment, hundreds of miles away, my wife smiles to herself. I clutch my hands to my chest and bend over weeping. I cry for a long time. For the first time in my life since Lana died, I feel complete.

From somewhere in the heavens, two angels smile down on me. I am a miracle. We all are. "I miss you Mom. I miss you Venus. You two watch over each other, I can handle things down here now."

# EPILOGUE

Sometimes I wonder how I made it through all these years on the journey of the disease of addiction. Heroin overdoses, State and Federal Prison sentences, lost relationships and broken hearts, homelessness, strained family ties, disgruntled and puzzled employers, dirty needles and questionable behavior, reckless driving, and the list goes on and on.

It has not been all bad news. I have survived, and I think that is the most important thing. I did not contract any STD, HIV, or Hepatitis. I have an excellent education and my mind is as sharp as ever. Most of the people I knew that journeyed down the same road as me have not been so fortunate.

I think the thing that hurts the most is that my mother never lived long enough to see me drug free. I was helpless to do anything for her in her time of need, while cancer slowly took her away from our family. I was off feeding my addiction when I should have been there for her and my family. Ironically, I feel that it was my mother, who somehow has brought me through this journey with nothing more than some deep emotional scars.

To all the living, who have suffered on either side of the fence, I leave you a piece of my soul. May you find some peace in your hearts on this journey called life. To all those who have left us, may you continue to be the whispers on the wind, for those who may someday hear your words of wisdom.

I miss you Mom…I miss you Venus. You will forever remain in my heart.

Mars